Mills & Boon
Best Seller Romance

A chance to read and collect some of the best-loved novels
from Mills & Boon – the world's largest publisher of romantic
fiction.

Every month, six titles by favourite Mills & Boon authors
will be re-published in the *Best Seller Romance* series.

A list of other titles in the *Best Seller Romance* series can be
found at the end of this book.

Kay Thorpe

CARIBBEAN ENCOUNTER

MILLS & BOON LIMITED
LONDON · TORONTO

First published 1976
Australian copyright 1983
Philippine copyright 1977
This edition 1983

© Kay Thorpe 1977

ISBN 0 263 74372 1

Set in Linotype Baskerville 10 on 11½ pt.
02—0783

Made and printed in Great Britain by
Richard Clay (The Chaucer Press) Ltd,
Bungay, Suffolk

CHAPTER ONE

THE building was long and low, pink-tinted against the brilliant blue sky at its back, the gold facia of its centre section glinting in the early afternoon sunlight. From her cabin porthole, Alex followed the waterfront along to the outer edge of a tree-shaded square where the San Juan taxi drivers parked their long American vehicles directly across the path most cruise passengers would take into the town proper, rising from there up the length of a narrow cobbled street which cut like a tunnel between close-packed buildings with overhanging balconies and crumbling façades until it finally gave way to the distant line of blue which was the sky.

With the port cover open the heat drifted in on a solid wave of humidity, fighting the air-conditioning of the cabin and bringing a faint beading of moisture to Alex's upper lip.

She closed it again, and turned back to view her home for the coming three months with the same sense of wonder that had kept her from becoming in any way blasé about her changing life-style over these last two years. It was still difficult to believe that she was actually here in Puerto Rico, half a world away from her normal haunts; even more difficult to see herself as the star attraction of the *Andromeda*'s Connaught Club Cabaret. The Connaught Line ships were renowned for the quality of their presentation in every sphere of shipboard life, and charged accordingly. Her audience here would consist of those used only to the best in life, and from her they would expect nothing less. For Barney's sake as much as for her own, she hoped she would be capable of rising to that expectation. He had put himself out on a limb getting her this job.

She smiled a little, remembering her very first meeting with Barney Wilson. Two years of steadily mounting success, first in the provinces and then in London itself, had gone a long way towards convincing her that he had not been talking through his hat that night so long ago, but she was also aware that without him she would still be nothing.

Pretty girls who could sing were ten a penny, he had told her somewhat brutally within a couple of minutes of their meeting, and her voice was no better than most. What she did have was a certain quality of expression which could be built into something sensational given a little help in technique. That was where he came in. If she did as he said, gave herself entirely into his hands, he would make her into star material. His life-lined features had taken on a wry cast at the doubt in her eyes. 'Look, kid,' he had added, 'you're an eyeful for any man, but I'm only interested in the voice. If you don't want to believe that just turn on round and walk right out of here.' Alex had believed it, and had never had cause to regret that trust. In Barney she had even found some replacement for the father she had barely known.

Alex's mother had died at her birth, and her relationship with her father had been at the best spasmodic. She had been twelve when he was killed on a mountain climbing expedition in the Himalayas, and she didn't suppose his death had made all that much difference to her life. She had gone on just as before, living in the home of the aunt who had brought her up, learning to accept the fact that genuine affection could not be bought with a monthly payment for her keep.

Her horizons had widened considerably once she had started work. By the time she was twenty she had found herself earning enough to leave her aunt's home to share a flat with two other girls from the same office. It was they who had encouraged her to render a few songs at parties after hearing her singing to herself in the bath, they who had pushed her into entering the talent contest which had eventually taken her forward to the televised final. She had come nowhere in that, but she had met Barney Wilson, the agent with a reputation for spotting winners before anyone else, and from then on she hadn't looked back.

Not that it had been easy. There had been times during the following weeks when she had wanted to walk out on the whole idea—times when the very sight of a sheet of music made her want to scream. But Barney wouldn't let her back out, using every means at his disposal to keep her chained to his bullying demands, to the point of demanding the return of money already invested in her forthcoming career. He had broken her down, torn her voice apart and then slowly built it up again into a sound which had a depth and timbre it had never achieved before. He had taught her how to move, how to use her hands, how to make every gesture a natural expression of the emotion she was putting across in her voice. He had made her learn the words of each new song like a piece of poetry before touching the music, to understand and appreciate what she was saying so that the emphasis came without forcing. Very, very rarely had he offered her a word of praise, so that the day when he had sat back on the piano stool and announced her ready for her debut had come as a complete surprise—even a shock.

That first engagement was in a Birmingham club,

and Alex had been far too nervous to remember much about it afterwards. All she did know was that the audience had seemed to like her. From then on it had been a steady progression upwards, learning all the time, gaining both in experience and confidence until she finally came to accept that her success was no fluke likely to vanish overnight, but a career opening up further and further ahead of her.

Yet surrounded by people as she always was, Alex had found herself oddly alone. Only with Barney could she feel truly at ease, and he had other artists to take care of as well as her. Meeting Ian Marriot in the park that lunchtime had seemed like the answer. They had been attuned from the beginning, identical in their likes and dislikes and both seemingly in need of a companion.

From meeting at lunchtime they had progressed to dinner on the nights when Alex wasn't working. On one or two occasions she had invited Ian back to her flat in Kensington for a late supper after a show, knowing she was on the verge of falling in love with him, and happy to have someone to care for who was completely divorced from the show business world. They had never discussed marriage, it was true; Alex had felt no immediate need to have their relationship on a firmer basis. The shock of discovering that Ian was already married had knocked her sideways nevertheless. Barney had been goodness itself during those following unhappy days, cancelling her engagements for the coming three months and presenting her with this cruise contract already tied up by way of giving her time to get over Ian. So here she was, Alex Gaynor, cabaret artist, hoping to mend a heart which if not exactly broken was certainly bent enough to still hurt.

It was time to get on with her unpacking. Walking across to the built-in dressing table, she saw the stiff white card propped up against the vase of flowers for the first time. It was a formal invitation to the Captain's table for dinner that evening. An honour indeed, thought Alex in some gratification. Now what did one wear on such an occasion?

The matching suitcases in cream leather awaited her attention on the specially provided racks close to the wardrobe. The whole cabin was beautifully appointed, with a thick-piled, rust-coloured carpet covering the floor edge to edge of the teak-fronted units. The bed lay against one bulkhead, made up for the day into a divan with bright orange and white covers which matched the curtaining looped back from the port.

Alex unlocked the larger of the three and found a couple of dresses, holding them up one by one in front of her to view her image in the long mirror set in the front of one sliding door. Her shoulder-length dark gold hair fell forward to frame a face which had attracted more than one assumption of mixed parentage. There was indeed a certain Italianate look about the slant of Alex's green eyes, in the high cheekbones and generous mouth, but there was nothing of Latin blood in her creamy, smooth-textured skin and slenderly curving figure. At one time she had deplored the five and a half feet which seemed to tower over her closer and somewhat shorter friends, but with Barney's aid she had learned to carry herself in a manner which made the most of everything she had. Her dress sense had been inborn. All she had needed was the wherewithal to indulge it to the full, and that she was on the way to acquiring.

The yellow silk tunic, she decided now, laying down

the other garment for the moment. It was floor-length and deceptively simple just held up as it was now, but on she knew that it fitted exactly where it should and looked every penny of its exorbitant price. This cruise was not like the usual kind where no one ever dressed to kill on the first night at sea. The *Andromeda* ploughed the Caribbean all the year round, dropping off passengers at one island and picking up others at another during the course of her weekly itinerary. Alex understood that she catered mostly for the American tourist trade, although she had noted a scattering of other nationalities among those milling around the main foyer when she had come aboard earlier. She hoped that some of the crew, at least, were British. It seemed likely on a British ship.

She was startled for a moment when the telephone rang. Somehow it didn't seem right to have a telephone system on board a ship, although what other form of communication might have been provided she had no idea. A liner was, after all, just a floating hotel.

The voice on the other end of the line sounded young and friendly and encouragingly welcoming. 'I'm Philip Osbourne, the Cruise Director's assistant. Nice to have you aboard, Miss Gaynor. I'm looking forward to hearing you sing.'

'Thanks,' she said, and meant it. 'I'm looking forward to getting started myself. Can you tell me what the arrangements are?'

'That's why I'm ringing. The Chief would like you to come to the Connaught Club at four for a run through some of your numbers with the orchestra. Will that be okay?'

It was already a quarter past three. This—Chief— whoever that was, obviously did not believe in wasting any time. Yet she was not due to open until Tuesday night with the first of her four performances per week. Surely there couldn't be such a tearing rush to rehearse?

'I'll be there,' she said after a brief moment during which she contemplated and rejected the idea of demurring. This was no time for any show of what might very well be taken for artistic temperament. In any case, it wasn't all that important when she rehearsed, now or later, provided she did so before going on. 'How do I find the Connaught Club?'

'It's on Connaught Deck, two decks above your own. If you turn to the left on leaving your cabin you'll come to the lifts. They'll bring you out behind the stage area. The Club is closed during the day, but the side door at the rear will be open for you. See you in a little while.'

Alex finished unpacking in less than half an hour, hanging away suits and dresses and filling the drawers with lingerie and beachwear. There was going to be plenty of opportunity during the coming months to use all that she had brought with her. Her spirits lightened considerably at that latter thought. Three months in the Caribbean, and paid for it too! Most folk would consider her a fortunate being indeed.

With everything neatly disposed of, she changed the light suit in which she had travelled for a pair of culottes in a silk print of black on white, fastening back her hair from her face with a matching bandeau. A pair of sling-back sandals in black completed the outfit. Ready and anticipatory, she caught up the slim leather satchel containing her musical arrangements and left the cabin in the direction Philip Osbourne had indicated.

She was alone in the lift. The ship was relatively

empty due to the absence of tourist parties on to the island, but those left on board suffered no shortage of entertainment judging from the daily intinerary of events she had seen in her cabin. In fact there were so many things going on that most must be hard put to decide what to do first. That would be part of the Cruise Director's job, she imagined, although no doubt what came across as good simple fun to the holiday-makers constituted a great deal of hard work and planning to him. She looked forward to meeting the kind of man who could successfully correlate so many different departments of entertainment.

The lift deposited her directly opposite the side door Philip Osbourne had spoken of. As promised it had been left open. Going through, she could hear the orchestra idly tuning up, and then she rounded the corner and came out into a long, luxuriously appointed room, with the stage and dance floor immediately on her left, and rows of velvet-upholstered couches fading off into the dimness of the unlighted rear reaches behind chrome and glass-topped tables. Two men in white tropical uniform of shirt and slacks stood with their backs turned towards her in front of the low stage talking with the orchestra leader. The latter was the first to see her, pausing in mid-sentence to impart the news to his companions.

The junior of the two officers must be the Philip Osbourne she had spoken to on the phone, she surmised as they both turned round. He was a very attractive young man with light brown hair swept back from a friendly open face. She gave him her warmest smile before transferring her attention to his companion, the former slowly fading before the calculated appraisal *he* was offering her. There was nothing either friendly or welcoming in the flinty grey eyes. Alex returned his gaze with an equanimity she was suddenly far from feeling, vitally aware of the strength of character in the lean, intelligent features. The Cruise Director was a man of no small stature, able to give her a good four inches even allowing for the three-inch heels she was wearing. She judged him still in his early thirties; younger than average, she would have imagined, to fill a job of this nature. Almost unconsciously she found herself noting the powerful breadth of his shoulders beneath the crisp white shirt, the clean finish of moderately styled dark hair.

'Welcome aboard, Miss Gaynor,' he offered formally without moving. 'I'm Clay Anderson. Sorry to call you so soon, but you're not going to have any further opportunity to work out with the full orchestra before Tuesday. They have a pretty full timetable.' He paused, glancing towards the man on the stage. 'You'll know Jimmy Keen by name.'

'And reputation.' Alex returned the older man's acknowledgement with genuine warmth. 'Working with the Keen orchestra is going to be a treat for me, Mr Keen.'

'You're not without a reputation yourself,' came the gratifying reply. 'Truth is, I'm a bit surprised to find you here on the *Andromeda* this winter. Rumour had it that you were all set for a season at the Blue Parrot.'

'Only second billing. My agent thought this might give me an edge on their next offer.'

He grinned. 'Trust Barney Wilson to know what he's doing! If that's what he thinks then you're in, girl!'

'Mind if we get started?' suggested the other man on an edge of impatience. 'I've got a Captain's reception to organise for seven-thirty.'

'Should be an established routine by now, I'd have thought.' James Keen's tone was mild.

The comment drew a faint, surprising grin. 'So should a whole lot of other events, but they rarely go to plan without a bit of urging. Let's say I'm taking no chances this week.' The grey eyes came round once more in Alex's direction, losing their humour in the process. 'Ready?'

She nodded without speaking, resenting his attitude but not prepared to let it throw her. The cause of his obvious antipathy puzzled as well as annoyed her. Maybe he thought her name not quite up to top billing in his precious cabaret, she reasoned, and was taking no pains to keep his opinion a secret. Well, the matter of her engagement had been decided by higher heads than his, and no amount of disapproval from him was going to rob her of it now. All the same, she found it impossible to ignore completely; the man himself was not the kind one could ignore. With some deliberation she focused the whole of her attention on James Keen, taking out the first three of her arrangements for his perusal as she stepped up on to the stage to join him.

In the following few minutes she could sense the growing restlessness in the man below, although nothing was said. If he was in such a rush there was no need for him to hang around anyway, was there? His job surely only covered the organisation of the cabaret, not the direction of individual acts. She would have liked to put that particular point to him, but doubted that it would serve any purpose to do so, other than to antagonise him even further. And not for him or for anyone else was she going to hurry through these vital moments of discussion with the orchestra leader. Above anything, it was essential that the two of them attained some measure of harmony from the start.

She began eventually with a standard that was one of her own favourites, feeling the delicious tension rising in her as she took up a casual position by the piano, ignoring the microphone for now. The pianist winked cheerfully at her, and without thinking about it she winked right back, responding to the camaraderie of a fellow performer. Then he was playing her introduction and James was cuing her in, and nothing else mattered but the job ahead.

Halfway through the number she broke off, shaking her head apologetically. 'Sorry, I seem to be lagging on the beat. Can you slow it down just a fraction?'

'Will do.' There was no hint of impatience in James Keen's voice. They were two professionals working towards a common aim—unison—no matter how long it took to achieve. 'From the top, boys!'

This time it was better. Alex felt herself relax into the feel of the song and knew that everything was going to be all right. As always the ballad caught her up in its emotional grip, blinding her to all but the need to express that same emotion in her voice. She didn't move away from the curve of the piano, continuing to lean with easy grace as she phrased the words, unaware of the picture she created against the dark polished wood. When she finished there was a brief pregnant silence before anyone spoke or moved. James Keen was the first to break it.

'You're going to make that billing,' he said simply, but it was more than enough.

Alex heard the murmur of approbation run through

the men grouped around her and felt the warm glow of pleasure only that kind of compliment could bring. Working with people like these was going to be sheer exhilaration these coming weeks. She could hardly wait to try out some of her more complicated arrangements.

It was several seconds before she recalled the audience out front. When she looked across it was to meet open admiration in the younger man's eyes, but Clay Anderson revealed no particular reaction either for or against. As their gazes clashed he got to his feet from one of the front couches and inclined his head towards the orchestra leader.

'I guess I can leave you all to it. Phil, you might make a note to cut that extra dance number we put in last month. I've a feeling we're not going to have to make up any time.'

Philip pulled a face. 'Are you going to tell Marian, or do I get that job too?'

His senior shrugged. 'I'll tell her myself if it bothers you that much. I'll be in my cabin for the next fifteen minutes if I'm wanted.'

'And good luck to him,' murmured the pianist, then grinned as he caught Alex's eye. 'With our Marian. She isn't going to like that cut one little bit, especially considering how she worked to get a solo spot in the first place. Hope your shoulders are broader than they look, because you're going to bear the brunt of it, if I'm any judge!'

Alex smiled. 'It won't be the first time. One thing I've learned this last couple of years is to grow a thick skin and take all that's offered with open hands. One person's luck has to be another's loss, I suppose.'

'True. Only in your case I'd say talent had as much to do with it.' The bony, almost ugly features held a look of sincerity. 'You've got what it takes, kid, like the man said.'

'Thanks.' Her voice was soft. 'You don't know how much that does for me.'

'If you've finished dishing out the mush maybe we can get on?' suggested Jimmy Keen, the twinkle in his eyes belying the satire of the words. 'How about trying out that blues number next?'

They worked for a further hour on the numbers Alex intended using during the coming week until they were both happy with the timing. By the time they did decide to pack it in she was tired, but satisfied with what they had achieved. Jimmy was as much of a perfectionist as she was herself, willing to go to infinite pains to get the right balance of sound. She was fortunate indeed to have someone like him to rely on.

Philip Osbourne had disappeared some time during the previous hour, but returned in time to congratulate Alex as she stepped down again from the stage. He was only a couple of years or so older than her own twenty-four, and quite devoid of any hint of his superior's brittle manner. The contrast alone was enough to create approval on her part.

'My cousin said you were good!' he announced with enthusiasm. 'He saw you in London during the summer. Actually, I expected you to be a bit older. Most of our established artists have been in the business for years.'

Alex laughed. 'It's an ageing way of life. I plan to retire at twenty-five myself.' She weighed the satchel in her hand and took a glance around. 'Is there anywhere I can get a long cool drink? My throat feels like the Sahara!'

'Sure. The Beach Deck bar is open right through.'

He added quickly, 'I'll show you, if you like.'

'That would be nice of you, providing I'm not taking up too much of your time.'

'I'm off duty right now, and I can't think of anything I'd rather be doing than buying Alex Gaynor her first drink on board.'

She was both amused and touched by his boyish eagerness. 'Fine, let's go.'

The sun terraces of the upper deck were well sprinkled with semi-naked bodies in various stages of burning under the sweltering sun. By now the shore parties would be beginning to return to the ship, although she was not due to sail until midnight. At present the pool seemed to be reserved for a children's session, with a dozen or so youngsters splashing happily about in it watched over by a couple of uniformed nursery staff. Alex caught a gaily coloured beachball which came flying towards her as they passed, ignoring the splatter of water to laughingly toss it back again.

'It will dry in seconds in this heat,' she assured Philip when he expressed concern for the damp patches down the front of her divided skirt. 'And the whole thing is quite washable.'

He smiled with her. 'You're not a bit like some of our star attractions.'

'So you keep telling me,' she returned on a light note. 'Maybe I'd better start thinking about my image a bit more.'

'You're great as you are.'

There was no mistaking the inflection in his voice. Alex stole a swift glance at his attractive profile and resolved to think twice before inviting any further compliments from this nice but far too vulnerable young officer. She had no conceit about her looks, but she was too sensible to underrate them either. Hers was a beauty which attracted attention wherever she went —an added asset for any performer, Barney had said from the start. Philip Osbourne wasn't the first to show signs of going overboard for her in a big way, and she had learned to steer clear of such complications: apart from Ian, of course. He had been different. In more ways than one, she reflected on an edge of cynicism. Still, it had taught her a lesson. From now on there were to be no emotional involvements outside of her work. As Barney had said, she couldn't afford the drain on her resources.

The Pool Bar held a scattering of people anxious to get into the shade for a while. Like everywhere else on board the luxury liner, it was beautifully fitted out. Alex sank gratefully into an upholstered swivel chair and took a long swallow of the iced Coke Philip had managed to procure within seconds of entering the place, then with her immediate thirst quenched she sat back and looked across at him.

'Tell me about yourself. How long have you been doing this job?'

'About four years. I was in the shipping offices before that.' He grinned a trifle sheepishly. 'I guess it was the glamour of the uniform that attracted me initially. Plus the fact that I'd always wanted to travel.'

'And?'

He shrugged. 'I've been on this run for twenty-three months. The same old routine week and week about. Any place gets monotonous once you've seen it a few times, I suppose.'

'Can't you apply for a transfer to another ship in the line?'

'I could, but why bother? The *Andromeda* is about the best berth to be had.'

'Worth a bit of boredom?'

'If anything is.' He looked back at her and lost the faint disgruntlement from his expression. 'Anyway, it isn't going to be boring *this* winter.'

Alex decided it was time to change the subject. 'Is Clay Anderson like that with all the performers you get on these cruises?' she asked on a casual note. 'Or is it just the females he doesn't like very much?'

'Clay?' Philip sounded surprised. 'I wouldn't say he had anything against women either on stage or off it. How do you mean?'

She studied him a moment, her brows creasing a little. Was it possible that no one else had noticed the Cruise Director's attitude in there? It seemed unlikely, thinking back, yet certainly no one else had revealed any hint of doing so. Doubt entered her mind. Maybe it was she herself who had read too much into too little, although she had never known herself overly sensitive that way before. She tried to recall the man's exact expression as he had watched her approach, and felt the doubts fade again. She wasn't wrong, she was sure of it. There had been contempt in that steely grey gaze. It bothered her more than she cared to admit. Why should a man she had never met in her life before feel that way about her?

'Oh, well, perhaps he just doesn't care for my kind of music,' she said lightly in an attempt to bring the whole business into perspective. 'One can't please all of the people all of the time. What's the Captain like? I've been invited to sit at his table at dinner tonight.'

Philip's descriptive powers were pretty fair, she discovered in some secret amusement several hours later. Captain Reginald D. Sylvester was straight out of Gilbert and Sullivan, and acting a lovely part. At the reception before dinner he had been photographed with almost every new passenger in the exact same pose, one hand lightly touching the edge of his formal mess-jacket to reveal the gold stripes of his command on the sleeve, leonine head slightly turned towards his companion or companions with a smile which said, 'Trust me to take care of you all' on his well-bred features. It was hardly fair, to pull him down for a little self-indulgence, however, she decided during the course of the superbly prepared and served meal. Running a vessel this size must place a tremendous weight of responsibility on those beautifully tailored shoulders. Who could blame him for needing to escape into another character on such occasions as this?

Two tables away Clay Anderson was presiding over a party of his own, at present deep in conversation with his left-hand partner, a woman in her late fifties who was lapping up the attention. Alex wondered if he too was allowed to choose his own dinner companions or must accept what circumstances and protocol thrust upon him.

With both her neighbours momentarily occupied with their farside partners she had time to study the firm profile of the man who so intrigued her. His kind of looks come under the classification of striking rather than handsome, the jaw rock-hard below a mouth which looked faintly sardonic even in repose, the nose straight and jutting, his hair slicked back by a ruthless hand. His hands were one of his most interesting features, perfectly in proportion to his size, yet with the long sensitive fingers of a musician or an artist: hands which could be either gentle or cruel, she imagined, depending on his mood. Some nameless emotion brought a momentary quiver deep down inside her, just as swiftly swamped by the confusion of lifting her eyes to find him looking straight back at her with a definite curl to his upper lip. She was infinitely grateful that her left-hand companion chose that very moment to turn back to her.

Philip claimed her the moment dinner was over, cutting her out from the rest of the party with a manœuvre she had to admire.

'I thought you might like to see something of the cabaret,' he said. 'It's due to start in about fifteen minutes. Then there's the Calypso Club, if you're not too tired. There's an excellent group up there, and they go on into the small hours. It's where all the real action is.'

Alex had felt tired earlier, but seemed to have got her second wind. Conscious of the necessity for caution where Philip was concerned, yet eager to sample all that the ship had to offer, she agreed to accompany him to the Connaught Club, but reserved her decision about the rest until later. She didn't even glance in Clay Anderson's direction as she left the restaurant with his junior, but she knew he was watching them. So let him look. So far as she knew there was no rule banning the cabaret artists from hobnobbing with the crew.

The orchestra was playing dance music when they reached the Club. Philip managed to secure a table close to the stage, and Alex smilingly acknowledged Jimmy Keen's wave. The cabaret began promptly at ten-thirty with a chorus line-up of six girls who would not have looked out of place among the Bluebells.

'That's Marian Lee centre left,' murmured Philip. 'Bet Clay hasn't told her yet!'

Alex followed the redheaded dancer with a new interest. She was an eye-catching figure in the brief, sequin-studded costume, with probably the best pair of legs in the whole line-up. They were all six excellent, but there was something about the redhead which put her just a little above the others.

'She's very good,' she murmured back. 'Attractive too!'

'A fair number of the crew would agree with you there. Only she's after Clay.'

Brave girl, thought Alex with satire.

There was only one other act that night, this time a conjurer with a unique line in magic using crystal globes, then the orchestra came back with a spot waltz which had many on their feet eager to win one of the cases of miniature whiskies constituting the prizes.

Philip pulled a comical face. 'Old hat stuff, this. Will you come up to the Calypso with me, instead?'

Alex made up her mind quickly. After all, she could hardly avoid Philip altogether, and he was quite old enough to look after his own interests without her trying to do it for him.

Reaching the other club she had to admit that Philip had had a point with regard to the action. The younger element obviously made this place their own from the word go. The setting was superb, this section of the uppermost deck jutting out for'ard like a cabin in the sky, its bulkheads set with large square ports which afforded breathtaking glimpses of the studded lights of city and coastline. The lighting inside was dim enough to create a sense of intimacy yet not too low for easy vision. He'd been right about the group too. Alex could feel the beat catching her up, making her itch to move with it.

Out of nowhere two other white-uniformed figures appeared to join them, and Philip gave a resigned sigh as he performed the introductions. The group switched without warning to a cha-cha-cha, and almost before she knew what was happening Alex found herself swept on to the floor by the assistant purser with typical Scottish informality.

Fortunately she was pretty adept at Latin-American dancing herself and within a couple of minutes had worked out her partner's somewhat complicated pattern of steps sufficiently well to follow him. Gradually others on the floor began to stand back, leaving the two of them space to move. Soon they were dancing alone within a cleared space of floor, the group entering into the spirit of the moment with gusto. Alex felt a little ostentatious, but would have felt even more so had she refused to continue. There was applause when they finally finished.

Laughing but definite, she declined to try out the next number with her exuberant partner, and walked off the floor to rejoin Philip. The hand on her arm just above the elbow came as a surprise which turned swiftly to dismay on meeting Clay Anderson's hard eyes as she turned to look at her accoster.

'There's something we have to discuss,' he stated. 'Out on deck, I think. Too much noise in here.'

Her former companion had vanished again into the crowd around the bar. Alex caught a glimpse of Philip through the press of bodies in their immediate vicinity, but he failed to spot her. She looked back at the man who still held her arm and lifted her shoulders. 'If you insist.'

He didn't bother to answer, drawing her along with him as he made for the rear of the thronged Club room. Then they were clear of the worst of the crush and exiting through a door into the night.

After the air-conditioned interior of the ship it was like stepping into a furnace. By unspoken agreement they moved across to the rails overlooking the lower section of the deck. Below them was a glint of water in the moonlight, the sound of laughter and a sudden splash as a body hit the surface of the pool.

'Perfect for a midnight swim,' commented Alex, forgetting for the moment who she was with and why. 'This heat is unbelievable!'

'I didn't get you out here to discuss the climate,' came the clipped response, and she stiffened.

'No, I don't suppose you did. What exactly was it you *did* want to talk about?'

'It's more in the nature of a piece of advice.' He paused, leaning an elbow along the rail, his expression hard and uncompromising. 'It no doubt amuses you no end to have all the men on board falling over themselves to be with you, but I'd stick to the single ones, if I were you.'

Alex drew in a slow breath, almost too taken aback to find any adequate reply. 'Are you talking about anyone in particular?' she said at length with fair control.

'The man you were just dancing with, for one—or should I say performing?' His mouth twisted. 'You can't stay out of the limelight for long, can you? Not that you're alone in that in your profession.' If he noted the angry glitter in her eyes it made no impression. 'Gerry Duncan has a wife and three kids he sees only one month in every four, and he's no less immune to temptation than any other man in similar circumstances. If you need your ego boosting young Philip seems more than ready to oblige, although I'd hardly place him in your league. Anyway, just steer clear of Duncan, that's all.'

'Is that an order?'

'If you like.'

'Too bad you don't have that kind of jurisdiction.' Alex wasn't all that certain that he didn't, if it came down to it, but she was too incensed to care either way. The utter injustice of his remarks stung in a way which aroused every warring instinct in her. For the first time in her life she knew what it felt like to want to slap a man's face with all her strength. 'Did it ever occur to you that your Scottish friend might not appreciate your concern for his welfare? I'd say he was old enough to make his own mistakes.'

'Old enough, but not too experienced in seeing them coming.'

'While you obviously are.' With some deliberation she infused an element of mockery into her tone. 'How old were you when you made *your* big mistake, Mr Anderson?'

His teeth came together with an audible sound. 'Another crack like that and I might just give way to my own inclinations. At least we'd be keeping it in the family!'

That brought her up short as nothing else could have done. Chest suddenly tight as a drum, she said, 'What are you trying to tell me?'

'That fact can be stranger than fiction any day of the week. Ian Marriot is my brother-in-law. It was my kid sister's marriage you messed up. Quite a coincidence isn't it?' There was a frightening viciousness in that latter question.

'I don't understand.' She was genuinely bewildered. 'Ian's wife didn't know about us. At least ...'

'She obviously found out. Now that I've met you I'm not sure I should attach as much blame to Ian as I have been doing either. He's only human.'

'Thanks!' The irony crackled.

His laugh was short and humourless, the glance he ran over her pointed. 'Why should I try to deny your looks? With that face and that body you're enough to turn any man on even before you open your mouth.' He caught the slight upward tilt of her lip and curled his own to correspond. 'Sure, including me. And I'm not married.'

'I'm not surprised.' She was trembling and doing everything she could to conceal that fact from him. 'You're taking it for granted that Ian and I ... that we had an affair?'

'What else would you call it?'

'What did *he* call it?'

'I didn't ask for the details.' His eyes narrowed. 'You expect me to believe it was purely platonic?'

'I don't expect you to believe anything but what you want to believe.' Alex had had enough—more than enough. The irony of the situation caught her by the throat. She had come all this way to forget about Ian, and now this! Fate, or pure coincidence? Not that it mattered which. Clay Anderson was right here on board the *Andromeda*, and would still be here when she left. That fact alone made the next three months seem more like three years. 'I'm going below,' she said.

He caught her by the shoulders as she made to turn away, pulling her back round towards him and holding her there. There was cruelty in the line of his mouth. 'Not quite so fast. I haven't finished yet.'

'What did you have in mind? A sample of what your
brother-in-law is supposed to have had? Sorry to dis-
appoint you, but it's been a long day.' The words were
spilling from her without consideration, born of the
need to hit back. 'Or maybe it's just that your own
attractions aren't quite what you imagine. Why don't
you go and find the woman you were with at dinner?
She looked more than ready to meet you halfway.'

For a brief moment he didn't move except for a faint
tensing of his jaw. Then, abruptly, he let her go.
'You're right. It's time you did get below before you
talk yourself into something you'll regret.'

Alex left him without another word, descending the
companionway to the lower deck and making her way
back inside to the lifts. Two minutes later she closed
the door of her cabin and stood there in the darkness
looking across to the uncurtained port and the star-
spangled night. They would be sailing in less than ten
minutes, she realised.

The anger of those moments up there on deck had
faded, leaving her weary and rueful. Had she been
offered a choice right then she would have packed her
things and left the ship without a moment's regret for
what she would be losing. But she didn't have that
choice. Not without letting Barney down all over
again. She was stuck with the situation just as it was.

CHAPTER TWO

THERE was ample opportunity during the course of the following few days for Alex to learn to find her way about the ship with ease. Despite her urge to see more of Venezuela than one could gleam from the La Guaira docks, she did not go ashore. Sightseeing could wait for the following week, or even the week after that: in three months they would call here at least twelve times. Meanwhile she had enough to occupy her mind right here on board.

She had seen little enough of Clay Anderson since the Saturday night, though she had not attempted to keep out of his way deliberately. She wondered once or twice if he himself was making that effort, but it seemed unlikely on the face of it. The ship was his province, and he was hardly likely to allow her presence to curtail his activities in any way. Alex tried to formulate the same attitude towards the whole business, but found it beyond her at present. She had been hurt and the wounds needed time to form a protective skin. By the time she did meet up with Clay again she wanted to be in full possession of all her emotions.

She was stretched out on one of the loungers on Beach Deck on the Tuesday afternoon when she became aware of being studied by the man occupying the chair set at right angles to her own. When she turned her head to glance his way he made no attempt to drop his eyes, but smiled and got up to come across and perch on the edge of the seat next to her.

'Hope you'll not mind me butting in on you,' he said. 'Only I was looking at your photograph down in the foyer earlier, and you're very recognisable. I'm Glenn Freeman. I understand we're to hear you sing tonight?'

'That's right.' Alex sat up a little straighter, tugging the straps of her bikini further up her shoulders again. 'Did you embark at San Juan too, Mr Freeman?'

'Yes. I'm with my daughter.' His tone was engagingly frank. 'A bit of a spur-of-the-moment idea really. I found myself with a spare few days and it seemed high time we started to get to know one another a bit better.'

Alex said shrewdly, 'And is it working out the way you hoped?'

A wry expression chased across his clean-cut features. 'I guess not. Maybe I left it too late. The two of us have been at loggerheads since we boarded. My own fault. I had visions of taking her round all the sights, but Sally seems more interested in staying on board with some of the other young folk she's met up with. Can't say that I blame her.'

'How old is she?'

'Seventeen.' His grin made him look suddenly younger than the forty-five or six years she had tentatively allocated him. 'And thinks she knows it all!'

'Didn't we all?' Alex felt herself drawn to the man in a way she could not have fully explained there and then. There was something solid and dependable about him. The fact that he also looked like every woman's dream of a high-powered American executive might have a little to do with it too, she conceded with faint self-mockery, and heard herself saying, 'Perhaps you should have brought your wife along to help bridge the gap.'

He shook his head. 'I've been a widower for twelve years. That's been the trouble, I suppose. I have to do a lot of travelling in my line of business, and that's meant we've never got to see a lot of one another. You could say Sally's been brought up by a succession of nannies. Could be this trip wasn't such a good idea. Might have been better if I'd taken her somewhere quieter where we could have been more on our own.'

It was Alex's turn to shake her head. 'I think that might have been even worse. At that age a girl needs to cut loose a bit in her own way.'

She had spoken reminiscently, and now she saw the interest deepen in Glenn Freeman's eyes. 'You sound as if you might have some personal feeling for this kind of situation.'

'In a way I have. I never had much time with my father either.' She hugged her knees, eyes narrowed against the glare of the lowering sun. 'You can't expect to just step into the role like putting on a new coat ... not in a week, at any rate.'

'I can't afford to take any longer than that right now.'

'You mean you still put your work before your daughter.' It was out before she thought about it. She bit her lip. 'Sorry, I had no right to say that.'

He was looking at her thoughtfully without resentment. 'Nothing to apologise for. I think you might very well be right. Habit is stronger than conscience, it seems.' There was a pause, then he said ruefully, 'You know, I didn't come across with any intention of talking about Sal at all. I just wanted to get acquainted.'

'Well, it did the trick, didn't it?' There was a glimmer of humour in her eyes, quickly reciprocated.

'I guess it did at that.' He glanced towards the bar on the far side of the pool. 'Can I get you a drink?'

'I'll have a Coke, please.'

'Nothing in it?'

She hesitated. 'Well, perhaps just a splash of Bacardi. I don't know whether it's to do with the heat, but alcohol seems double strength out here.'

Glenn grinned. 'Not double strength, just double measures. Saves time and glasses.' He stood up with a suppleness which belied the sprinkling of grey among his reddish-brown hair. 'Don't go away.'

Alex watched him walk round the pool, noting the way he carried his tall spare frame. Hers were not the only feminine eyes to follow him either. Some instinct caused her to lift her gaze towards the upper deck where she had stood with the Cruise Director three nights before, and she felt her whole body tauten at the sight of the uniformed figure standing in the very same spot. He was looking straight at her, mouth pulled into a thin line. How long he had been standing there she had no idea, but it was obviously long enough for him to have formed his own impressions of her chat with Glenn. She resisted the impulse to wave a mocking hand. Why make things any worse than they already were?

He had gone by the time Glenn returned, but the incident left a tension which made it impossible to relax with the American as she had before, although she tried not to let him see it.

'I'll look forward to hearing you tonight,' he said when she finally announced that she must go and change. 'Perhaps you'll join Sally and me for a little while after the show? I'm sure she'd be thrilled to meet you.'

Alex had reservations on that score, but she kept them to herself. 'I'd like that.'

'So would I.' He gave her a hand to her feet, holding on to it for a moment as though reluctant to let her out of his sight. 'I'll be counting the hours.'

Philip was emerging from the inner regions of the ship as she made her way aft.

'Hi,' he greeted her, face lighting up. 'Haven't seen you around all day.'

'I've been on the sun terrace.' Her smile was pleasant but not designed to encourage. 'I'm on my way down to get changed. You look harassed.'

'Card party. We just got through putting back the tables. There's horse racing in the Cavendish Room at half past four, if you're interested.'

She wrinkled her nose. '*Horse* racing?'

'Cardboard cutouts and drawing from the hat for each move. Not bad fun. Why don't you come along when you've changed?'

'I don't think so, thanks. I've got some letters to write.' She smiled again and made to pass him. 'See you.'

'I thought we might try the Calypso again after the show tonight.'

'Sorry.' She was grateful for a genuine reason to refuse. 'I'm afraid I'm already booked. Some other time, perhaps?'

'Yes, sure.' He looked so crestfallen that she was almost tempted to suggest the following evening, but common sense held her back. Philip was the type to get serious with very little encouragement, and she had more than enough on her plate without that.

She made her escape before he could come up with any other ideas.

A shower and a change into a light linen dress refreshed her enough to be able to contemplate her coming debut later that evening with rather more equanimity than she had known all day. No matter how often she opened in a new place it was always like the very first time all over again. The time to worry, Barney always said, was if she stopped suffering from any kind of nervous tension at all, because that would mean the

onset of complacency regarding her talents. Alex wished
he could be here with her now; just to see his leathery
face would be all that she needed. He had held her
hand on all such other occasions; perhaps more than he
should have done. It was time she learned to stand
entirely on her own feet, like a real professional, and
here was her ideal opportunity.

The table to which she had been allocated in the
restaurant was shared with an elderly American couple
taking their half-yearly cruise on the *Andromeda*, and a
young Venezuelan pair so wrapped up in one another
Alex was sure they must be on their honeymoon. The
latter spoke very little English anyway, so most conversational gambits took place among the three of
them.

'So this is your opening night,' said Lawrence Miller
when they were all seated for dinner. 'We'll have to go
and get ourselves some good seats for the show before
everybody gets the same idea, eh, Lucille? Can't afford
to miss the little lady's performance. What time will you
be on?'

'About eleven,' Alex told him. 'But Friday's will be
the more elaborate cabaret. It's Carnival night, isn't
it?'

'Sure is,' Lucille Miller agreed comfortably. 'I always
enjoy wearing those flowery things round my neck.
Leis, I believe they're called. Really belongs to the
Pacific islands, that custom, but nobody cares. I hope
everything goes okay for you, honey. We'll be out there
rooting for you.'

Alex thanked the two of them gratefully. It helped to
know there was *someone* out there. At the back of her
mind was the hope that Clay Anderson would not find
it necessary to put in an appearance at tonight's show,

though it was a pretty forlorn one. It would be a part of his job to keep an eye on the way things were going, particularly in the case of a comparatively unknown quantity like herself.

She had already deposited her dress and make-up in the dressing room she had been allocated to the rear of the Connaught Club stage, leaving herself with over an hour to kill after she had finished her meal before it would be time to prepare for her own part in the evening's show. Ascending to the upper deck, she could hear the orchestra playing dance music to a Latin-American tempo, and knew then that she would probably never hear that rhythm again without remembering her first night on board the *Andromeda*. One thing was certain, she would not be able to get through the whole three months of her engagement without clashing with Clay again. She doubted if he would even have considered letting the matter rest. So far as he was concerned she was nothing but a little tramp who deserved to have her nose rubbed in the dirt—and he wouldn't be loth to do the rubbing either, should she provide him with the opportunity. But he wasn't going to get that opportunity, she promised herself tautly. If he made so much as an attempt to lay his hands on her again she would make a complaint—to the Captain himself, if necessary. Drastic as it seemed, the decision cheered her.

At this hour the upper terraces of Beach Deck were empty. Alex found a chair close by the spot where she had spent the afternoon and sat watching the long slow roll of the sea out there under the moonlight, seeing the phosphorus shimmering over the curling head of the bow wave. Tension built up slowly within her as the minutes ticked by, her nerves stretching with a sensation that was both painful and pleasurable at the same time. Her throat felt too dry to be capable of producing any kind of note, but she was too well accustomed to that particular symptom to let it bother her. When the time came her muscles would relax; they always did. This was the worst part: the build-up; the waiting and wondering as to how she would go down. This was an American majority audience, and she had never sung to such before. Supposing they didn't like her?

Then you'll darn well *make* them like you, she told herself firmly at that point.

There were four cabins in use as dressing rooms for the artists. Marian Lee was alone in the one next door to Alex's when she went down, with the door wide open. She gave Alex a hard glance before leaning forward to push it closed with unnecessary force, leaving the other girl to shrug her shoulders a little wryly and walk on. Obviously the dancer had been told of her loss of the solo spot and didn't like it. Alex couldn't really blame her, but would have preferred not to have been granted the role of scapegoat. In all probability, Clay had seen no reason to exclude her from responsibility for the cancellation; he might even have intimated that she had demanded the extra time. She would put nothing past a man of his kind. Not that it was so important now. She had met professional enmity before this.

She was struggling to do up the long back zip of her figure-hugging emerald gown when the tap came on the door. Expecting the stewardess with the coffee she had ordered, she called 'Come in,' without bothering to turn round from the mirror, then froze as her caller came into view.

'What do *you* want?' she demanded.

'Just checking.' There was a mocking inflection in the words. 'Having trouble?'

'Nothing I can't handle, thanks.' She saw him start to move closer, and whipped round to face him, sending a jar of cold cream spinning to the floor with her free hand. 'Get out of here!'

He bent down and retrieved the jar, placing it back in its former position on the dressing table. 'Lucky it didn't break. I'll give you a hand with that zip.'

'I said get out.' Alex backed away up against the table, conscious of the low neckline of her dress falling away from her shoulders as she let go of the material she had been holding together at the back. 'I don't need any help from you.'

'You need it from somebody, and I seem to be all that's available at present.' His eyes held a challenge. 'Are you going to turn round and let me do you up, or do you plan to take your bows holding on to your modesty? You're on in five minutes.'

She looked at him for a full five seconds before turning with an abrupt movement to stand waiting rigidly for his attention. The mirror reflected his sardonically tilted mouth as he stepped up behind her, then there came the light touch of his fingers against her skin and she drew in a sharp little breath. Grey eyes found hers in the mirror, their expression only too easy to read. Alex dug her nails into the palms of her hands, despising herself for that involuntary response to the brief contact. Now he had another weapon to use against her—and he knew it.

She wanted to jerk away from him the moment the zip was safely up, but she forced herself to stay exactly as she was. To move now would be to acknowledge his effect on her, and that was one satisfaction he was not going to get.

'Thanks,' she said.

'Any time.' He still hadn't taken his eyes from hers. It took a second knock on the door and the rattle of china to break the deadlock. Alex was aware of relief as she invited the stewardess to enter.

If the newcomer was surprised to find the Cruise Director in the star dressing room she gave no sign, simply placing the tray ready for Alex and departing again with businesslike efficiency. Clay had moved off a couple of paces before the intrusion. Now he followed her to the door, pausing there to glance back at Alex with a thin-lipped smile before going out.

Her hand was unsteady as she poured the coffee. She took it strong and black, grateful that it wasn't hot enough to burn her mouth as she gulped it down. Right at the moment she could have done with something rather more potent, although alcohol was not the best of stimulants on which to perform. Damn the man! What right had he to come in here like that? And what was wrong with her that she could feel any kind of response at all to someone who had said the things he had said to her? Basic chemistry, she told herself in an attempt at mitigation: an automatic physical reaction which had nothing at all to do with one's feelings towards a person. Only she doubted if the man who had just left would see it quite that way; a physical relationship appeared to be the only kind he recognized between a man and a woman.

Remembering the calculating gleam in his eyes, she gave a small shiver. A man like Clay Anderson would more than likely consider it mere poetic justice to take full advantage of any opportunity to pay her back in her own supposed coin. But he was barking up the wrong tree if he thought she could be drawn into *any* kind of relationship with him. From now on she stayed at as great a distance from him as she could manage within the confines of the ship.

Standing in the darkness to one side of the cleared and spotlit floor some moments later, she closed her mind to all thoughts of what had happened previously to concentrate on the man introducing her. She heard his final build-up through the rapid timing of her heartbeats, the sound of her name; and then the first notes of her opening number were drawing her forward into the blaze of the spotlights on light dancing feet to take the hand mike out of the compère's outstretched hand and direct a glowing smile towards the sea of faces reaching back into the darkness as she went straight into the catchy rhythm over the top of the welcoming applause.

That first song went down well enough to lend her all the encouragement she needed to let herself go. In twenty minutes she worked through four more numbers, interspaced with the gay, inconsequential chat Barney had taught her to put across. For a finale she was using the ballad she had sung on her initial workout with the orchestra, this time leaning against one of the pillars supporting the deck above, with a single spot outlining just her face and shoulders.

The change over from a fast number to a slow involved more than a mere adjustment of tempo: it meant a switch of mood as well. Alex did it by detaching her mind from all audience distractions to dwell only on the words she was about to put to music, starting off soft and low and letting the phrasing come to her instead of going after it. A pin could have been heard to drop in the crowded club within a moment or two of her opening her mouth, a stillness continuing for several seconds after the last semi-whispered note before erupting into a storm of wildly applauding hands.

'You'll have to give them an encore,' murmured Jimmy Keen as she hovered in front of the stage to acknowledge the undiminishing ovation. 'How about "Cabaret"?'

At that moment there couldn't have been a more appropriate choice. Alex thrilled to the sudden increase in volume as the orchestra played her in, just as quickly hushed for the opening bars of the song made famous by one of their own leading singers. They liked her. They really liked her! It was the most wonderful feeling in the world!

There were congratulations waiting from other performers when she eventually came off. Safely back in her dressing room, she took a few moments to let the adrenalin settle before starting to change back into her other self. Her eyes in the mirror were brilliant and excited. She knew it would be some time before the tingling elation began to die down.

Eventually, dressed once more in the simple blue gown she had worn at dinner, she left the dressing room and made her way through to the club bar to join Glenn and his daughter. He was waiting for her at a table close by the rear doors leading through to the foyer, but he was alone.

'You were superb,' he said as she came up. He pulled out a chair for her with some small pride of possession in the way he hovered over her for a moment before regaining his own seat. 'Did you ever sing in the States?'

She shook her head with a smile. 'I'm not an international star, despite the claims in the brochures. My agent used his influence to get me this particular job because he believes it will be of help to me later on. The *Andromeda* is a very exclusive ship.'

'I suppose it is. And I'm sure you're very soon going to be in demand over our side of the Atlantic. I'll pull every string I can to get you there.'

She was intrigued. 'Are you involved with the show business world?'

His shrug was light. 'Let's just say I have enough contacts among the top brass for my word to carry a little weight, especially when your success here gets back via word of mouth. They all went for you in a big way out there tonight.'

'Yes, they were wonderful.' Experience had taught Alex never to indulge in false modesty regarding her impact on an audience. She knew that she had made a good start, and it was unlikely that she would know any failure from here on in, unless she was unfortunate enough to run into a majority group of entirely different tastes from the present clientele. At the same time it was necessary to make allowances for the fact that all of those people out there tonight were on vacation and therefore rather less inclined to be critical than any audience paying separately for tickets to hear an artist perform. The possibility of an American contract in the not too distant future was both exciting and frightening. But not to count her chickens before they were hatched. No matter how many people she had pulling for her it had to depend ultimately on her likely drawing power on the American circuits.

'Is your daughter joining us?' she asked, and saw a different expression cross her companion's features.

'I'm afraid not. She's gone to the discothèque with some friends.'

'Well, that's understandable. I don't suppose she finds this kind of thing quite her cup of tea.' Alex waited a moment before adding softly, 'You're worried about her, aren't you?'

'A little,' he admitted. 'I know girls of seventeen are grown-up these days, but Sally's always been rather on the quiet side. She likes reading and going to concerts mostly. I didn't even know she knew any of these modern dances.'

Alex laughed. 'You don't have to know any particular steps, just throw yourself into the beat. Anyone can do it within a few minutes providing they're not shy to let themselves go a little. It's a great deal easier than jive.'

He grinned back at her. 'You're too young to know anything about the jive era.'

'There have been several attempts to revive it lately.'

'Well, at least it was a contact type dancing. Today's stuff you could do on your own without anyone being any the wiser.'

She glanced at him obliquely. 'Safer, though, wouldn't you say?'

He got her meaning right away. 'You could be right. I suppose I should be grateful the real old clinching style went out. There was nothing scheduled to heat up the blood quicker than a dreamy waltz on a crowded floor with all those spinning lights and other shemozzle. I met my wife that way.'

'Have you never considered getting married again?' she asked, hearing the subtle change in his voice.

'Never met anyone else I wanted to marry.' His vivid blue gaze sought hers and as swiftly dropped again. 'By the time you reach my age you're pretty set in your ways. The problem might be finding a woman willing to take me on now.'

'You're talking as if you were approaching senility,' she chided lightly. 'You can't be more than forty-five.'

'You're out by three years. I'm forty-eight.' Once again his eyes found hers. 'More than old enough to be *your* father too. Do you mind having an old man as your date?'

'I shall if you keep calling yourself that, even in a joke. Being old has nothing to do with years.' She was thinking of Barney Wilson as she said it. 'One of the youngest men I know will never see sixty again.'

'That's a great outlook. Gives a man a real boost!' He was smiling. 'From now on I'll concentrate on feeling young.'

They had another drink and chatted for a while after that. It was Alex who eventually put in the casual suggestion that they should take a stroll along Beach Deck, sensing Glenn's slight preoccupation. If he could just catch a glimpse of his daughter it might ease his mind.

The beat of music reached them as they came out into the open air. Alex saw Glenn glance up the short companionway in the direction of the glass doors leading through into the Calypso Club, but he made no attempt to steer her in that direction. She thought she understood his dilemma. Should Sally catch a glimpse of him anywhere near the club she would probably take it that he was spying on her, that he didn't trust her to behave out of his sight. It was a difficult situation, and Glenn had no previous experience of such. Alex tried to imagine how she would have felt at seventeen under the same circumstances, but could only come to the conclusion that she would personally have welcomed *any* kind of display of concern for her welfare on her father's part. Not that she had had much opportunity to make contact with people of her own age at that time; her aunt had kept her rather restricted as to hours of freedom. Perhaps partly because she was someone else's child and therefore even more of a responsibility than one's own. Anyway, nothing in her own experience could help her suggest a possible course of action to Glenn now. He would have to sort out his family affairs by himself.

A dark blur against the rails further along the deck resolved itself into a couple intertwined in what looked at a distance like a fairly passionate embrace. Then, suddenly, one of the figures was pushing itself away from the other, and a young voice was heard raised in protest. 'No, don't!'

Glenn gave a sharp exclamation and was gone from Alex's side, striding forward to confront the man even now reaching out to grasp the girl by the arms and pull her towards him again. 'I mean you no harm,' Alex heard him say in a heavy accent. 'You like to play games, eh?'

'Leave her alone!' Glenn was apparently ready to emphasise the words with a fist, judging from the way they were clenched. 'Sally, come away from that ... gigolo!'

At any other time Alex might have found the antiquated term amusing, but right now there seemed nothing at all to laugh at. The Venezuelan—or so she took him to be—had turned to meet his accoster with a belligerence quickly squashed by the other's obvious acquaintance with his young friend. He was a rather superb specimen of South American manhood, Alex had to concede, still in his early twenties, with the

muscular grace of an athlete and an arrogantly handsome face beneath the thick sweep of black hair. Even
in transferring his gaze from one Freeman to the other,
he managed to run a quick appraising glance over her
standing quietly in the background.

'I apologise,' he said without hesitation to Glenn. 'I
was not aware that Sally was here with anyone else or I
would not have agreed to bring her out on deck.'

'It was you who suggested it!' The latter's pretty
young face held indignation. 'And you promised not
to . . . not to do anything.'

'I did nothing,' came the swift protest. 'A kiss in the
moonlight is not in my country considered a crime.'
His eyes came back to Glenn with a plea for male
understanding. 'You must believe me, I did . . .'

Glenn said tersely, 'If I see you anywhere near my
daughter again this trip I'll have you put off the ship.
Get going!'

The younger man left, though without haste, his eyes
once again sliding over Alex in passing with unconcealed approval. Sally was looking anywhere but at her
father, her mouth fairly trembling but mutinous too
in the moonlight. She was a very attractive girl, long
slim legs bare beneath the short white dress, dark hair
tumbled about her averted face. Glenn seemed uncertain of how to handle the situation, and because of it
took refuge in anger.

'Haven't you any more sense than to come out here
with a guy like that?' he demanded. 'His kind only
wants . . .'

'I didn't know he was going to try anything. He was
so nice to know when we were dancing.' Sally sounded
close to tears. 'He—He bought me a drink and . . .'

'What kind of drink?'

'A lime juice. You know that's all I like.' This time she did manage to look at him, relief struggling with resentment in her voice. 'Did you come up here to look for me?'

'No, I wanted a breath of fresh air.' A bit far-fetched, Alex reflected even as she said it, considering the beautifully conditioned air of the ship's interior, but beggars couldn't be choosers. She moved forward. 'I'm Alex Gaynor. Your father and I met up here this afternoon.'

'Yes, he told me.' Sally was obviously grateful for the interruption but uncertain of her ground. 'I'm sorry about not coming to the show.'

'I like dancing too,' Alex returned without undue emphasis. 'I do another on Thursday, but the best one will be Carnival night on Friday. Perhaps you and your father will come together then?'

'Yes, I'd like to.' Sally hesitated, glancing again at the tall, white-jacketed figure between them. 'I think I'll go down to bed. Will you ... Will you come down with me?'

She was afraid of running into the Venezuelan again, Alex surmised, and took the initiative without pause for reflection. 'Yes, do, Glenn. I'll be turning in myself in a minute or two.'

'We'll see you to your cabin,' he offered, but she shook her head.

'I'll take a turn around the deck first, or I shan't sleep. I always need to run down after a performance and I can do it better alone.'

The Pool Bar was still open for business the length of the pool away from where they stood, with several customers plainly visible behind its widely flung doors. Had it not been for that Alex had the feeling that Glenn would not have been prepared to leave her

alone on deck, but as it was he finally nodded, albeit
with reluctance.

'Are you booked on an excursion when we reach
Barbados tomorrow?' he asked, and then as she shook
her head, 'Then perhaps you'll give us both the
pleasure of your company on a tour of the island? I've
arranged for a car to be waiting at nine-thirty on the
dock.'

'Yes, do come!' Sally sounded convincingly eager.
'Barbados is one place I really do want to see. I've
heard so much about it from friends who've been there
on vacation.'

'Thank you, I'd love to come.' Alex really meant it.
The Freemans showed signs of needing some third person to act as something of a buffer while they worked
out a closer understanding. She already liked Glenn a
great deal, and was sure she would get along with Sally
too. And it was more than time she got off the ship for
a break from what was fast becoming routine. 'Can I
meet you at the gangway?'

'Please.' Glenn still hesitated, reluctant to leave her
yet conscious of his daughter's prior claim. 'We'll be
looking for you.'

Alone again, Alex moved slowly aft, trailing a hand
along the rail as she went. She would give Glenn and
Sally time to gain the lifts and then she would go down
herself. She had spoken the truth in stating that she
needed to run down before sleep would come, but the
star-spangled sky and moonlit seascape were hardly
scheduled to create the kind of mood she required.
There was a restless sensation deep down inside her, a
yearning she refused to put a name to.

Over on the far side of the deck a blur of white
merged with the superstructure and stayed there. One

of the officers doing a duty prowl, she surmised, and terminated that line of thought before memory could summon disturbing images to mind. When the other figure moved out of the shadow of the companionway before her she felt her heart give one almighty thud before she recognised the dark features of the man Glenn had despatched on his way some few minutes earlier.

'You stay here alone,' he observed with a smiling intonation that needed no interpretation. 'You know I will wait for you to get rid of your friend after the way we look at each other, yes?'

His confident audacity took Alex's breath away. The way they had looked at each *other*! She eyed the bold features with a sudden desire to giggle; probably the result of nerves. There had been plenty of times in the past when she had found it necessary to freeze off a would-be suitor, but never before had she been faced with quite such calm assurance of reciprocation on her part.

'I think you're taking a little too much for granted,' she said. 'I was about to go down to my cabin.'

'Your cabin or my own, it is of little consequence. We are of the same mind, eh, *querida*? I knew when I saw you that here was a real woman, not like the other. She was so very pretty but not, I think, very experienced in the ways of men.'

'She's seventeen,' Alex responded tautly, and he lifted a surprised brow.

'So much? I would have believed her younger. In my country ...'

'In your country the customs are obviously far different from ours.' The comment was sharp. 'You must be about the most conceited male on board!'

His teeth gleamed in amusement without any hint of deflation. 'I have much to be proud of. Many of the girls up there,' indicating the higher deck, 'would like to be with Chico Varagas tonight, but I choose you!'

'Then you can unchoose again, because I'm not available.' Alex was quite unable to take the situation with any real seriousness. 'Goodnight, Señor Varagas.'

He moved ahead of her as she made to pass him to enter the body of the ship, his smile undiminished. 'You do not mean that. You want me to persuade you, that's right?' He didn't bother to wait for an answer. 'Then I persuade you!'

Alex put up both hands to fend off his enthusiastic advance, felt them brushed aside and was next moment pinned against the bulkhead with the dark face looming over her. But only for a moment, then as if by magic the confining body was whirled away from her and Clay Anderson appeared in her line of vision, his face set in lines which boded ill for the Venezuelan should he not take the hint. The latter's expression was a study. Twice inside half an hour was too much! Without a word he turned and vanished inside via the door Alex herself had been about to use.

Eyeing her rescuer, she knew exactly how Sally had felt. She was grateful to him for extracting her from what had threatened to become a rather sticky moment, but no amount of gratitude could blind her to the look on his face. He might have come to her aid because that was part of his duty as a ship's officer, only there was no doubt in her mind that he considered the whole affair at least partially her own fault for being up here alone in the first place.

His first words seemed to confirm that impression. 'Our shipboard Romeos aren't always able to tell vic-

tims from reciprocants. I daresay a woman alone repre-
sents a fair invitation. What were you hoping to
prove?'

She glanced at him sharply. 'I don't think I understand.'

'It shouldn't be too difficult. You must have known
he was still hanging around when you decided not to
accompany your friends.'

'You were watching?'

'The whole thing. I'd seen the two of them come on
down from the Club, and noticed the girl's age—or lack
of it, in this case. If you and her father hadn't come on
the scene when you did I'd have gone across and broken
it up myself.' His lips twisted satirically. 'We're here
to protect both the weak and the foolish.'

Which heading did she come under in his estimation? Alex wondered, and could find nothing to say
other than, 'How did you know he's her father?'

'He's too old to be her brother, and the relationship
is obviously family. Call it a natural conclusion.' He
paused. 'If it comes to that, he must be twenty-five years
older than you are.'

'Twenty-four, if we're going to be down-to-earth.'
With irony she tagged on, 'And we are going to be
down-to-earth, I take it?'

'If I told you ...' He broke off, driving his hands
down into his pockets with a force which suggested
deliberate control. 'Freeman, I believe his name is?
One of the bigger fishes on board, I'll give you that.
You don't waste much time in sorting out the pool!'

'You don't seem to have done much time-wasting
yourself.' She was determined not to let him get
through her barriers. 'What doth it profit a man to be
richer than his neighbours on board *Andromeda*?'

Grey eyes narrowed dangerously. 'What are you getting at?'

'It shouldn't be too difficult,' she mimicked, and felt a quick thrill of alarm run through her as his hands came out of his pockets again. Common sense told her to stop right there, but something stronger drove her on regardless. 'Call it a natural conclusion.'

That was as far as she did get. One minute he was standing there a few feet in front of her, the next she once more had her back against the hard bulkhead with a man's arms blocking her escape. Only this time there was no one available to cut the scene short. Alex went rigid as his mouth found hers, unable to struggle within the hard circle of his grasp, her whole body alive to the close-bound contact. She had been kissed plenty of times before, but never with such punishing brutality. For the first time in her life she knew what it was like to be powerless against male strength and purpose, and it wasn't a feeling she liked. When he finally lifted his head she made a blind attempt to get a hand up to his face and rake her nails down it, but he still had too secure a hold on her.

'You take a swing at me,' he threatened softly, 'and I'll swing right back!'

He meant it too; she didn't doubt that for a second. She subsided, eyes blazing into his. 'Get your hands off me!'

'When I'm good and ready.' His arms slackened, but only enough to let her back against the bulkhead again. 'It's time somebody put you where you belong.'

'Just me, or all women?' she flashed, and saw his mouth pull into a slow smile.

'That reached you, at any rate. If Nature had intended us to be equal she'd have given you a different shape. And don't try sidetracking. Equality isn't the issue at stake.'

'Then what is?'

'Fidelity, if you like.' He had a hand resting against the metal either side of her now, not touching her yet not allowing her freedom. 'You denied anything physical between you and Ian the other night. Was that supposed to mean he never tried to make love to you, or that you refused to let him?' His voice roughened when she failed to answer. 'Go on, tell me he never even kissed you. I've heard taller stories.'

'Yes, he kissed me. And I let him. Why shouldn't I, when . . .'

'Because he already had a wife, that's why. Didn't you ever think of *her*?'

'I didn't . . .' She stopped abruptly, pride refusing to allow her any explanations. He wouldn't believe her anyway. He had made it plain that he would believe nothing she told him. Chin lifted, she gave him back look for look. 'No,' she said, 'I'm afraid I didn't. Is there really any point in talking about it any further?'

It was a moment before he answered, an undecipherable expression coming and going in his eyes. 'I daresay not. The damage is already done.' He straightened then, giving her room to move. 'I'll see you down to your cabin.'

'I'll manage on my own.'

'I said I'll see you down. Romeo might just have taken it into his head to lie in wait for you. His kind doesn't take no for an answer easily.'

He wasn't the only one, she reflected, but refrained from voicing that particular sentiment. The way things were it was safer just to go along with him for the moment.

There was no sign of the Venezuelan when they went in to take the lift down to Atlantic Deck. Clay greeted the people already occupying the cage with pleasant informality and stood there at Alex's side while they descended, apparently unaware of the curious glances they were attracting. He didn't bother to speak at all until they reached her cabin. There, he asked for her key and opened the door, reaching in to switch on the light before standing back to allow her entry.

'Safe and sound,' he said. 'You're luckier than you realise.'

He was gone before she could think of any adequate reply.

CHAPTER THREE

THE tour of Barbados with Glenn and Sally came as a light relief to Alex after the events of the previous night. The island captured her imagination with its curving white beaches and brilliant tropical colours, its cheerful, friendly populace. They would all have liked to spend longer there, but with only the one day they had to make the most of the best of it, relying on the hired driver's idea of what constituted that latter. He was a delight in himself, full of Bajan wit and highly conscious of his position as guide. 'You folk wanna listen or go back there knowin' nuthin'?' he queried irately at one point when their comments on the scenery overrode his own, and like lambs they shut up, Sally stifling her giggles behind a clenched fist.

They had lunch at Sam Lord's Castle on the south-east coast, revelling in the Regency atmosphere of mirrored walls and ornate ceilings. Samuel Hall Lord had built the place in a fit of nostalgia for his home-land during the first part of the last century, and it had been a museum when the present owner had seen its potential as a hotel. Today, it was reputed to be among the most beautiful in the world, set among sloping, sun-washed lawns overlooking the sea. The servants still wore Regency livery with a crest of horned swans, but there was nothing servile in the smiling countenances of those who waited on table.

'Imagine living in a place like that,' sighed Sally on the way back to the ship. 'I'll bet this Samuel Lord was a real cutie!'

'According to legend he was a buccaneer, even a murderer,' put in her father dryly. 'But I agree about the house. Perhaps we could take another trip down this way before too long and stay there ourselves.'

'Alex too?' The question was lightly put.

Alex smiled and said with equal lightness, 'I don't think I'll be seeing the Caribbean again for quite some time after I finish this cruise contract. My agent is planning all sorts of things for when I get back.'

Glenn gave her a quick glance. 'You've heard from him?'

'This morning.' She looked out of the window at the waving casuarinas lining the road, green heads reach-ing far into the blue, at the vibrant colours of the flowers overflowing from every garden large and small alike. 'It's raining in London ... at least, it was when

Barney wrote his letter. It all seems so far away. I can hardly imagine being cold again.'

'No, it certainly is a dandy place to spend a winter,' Glenn agreed. 'Can't think why I didn't make it before this.'

'You were always too busy before,' Sally said matter-of-factly, and he grimaced.

'I suppose that's right. Well, I'll just have to make sure I don't get that way again, won't I?'

Her smile was reserved, as though she only half believed it. 'Yes.'

It somehow seemed to be taken for granted that Alex should spend both her days and her evenings with the Freemans after that. She didn't mind. She was coming to like both father and daughter a great deal, and it kept her out of Clay's way. On several occasions she observed the latter watching her when she was alone with Glenn, but he never attempted to intrude or to contact her in any way. Yet he hadn't finished with her either, she was sure of that. It wasn't in him to let her off the hook so easily. Sooner or later they were going to clash again. Alex found the waiting almost worse than the actuality.

Martinique proved a complete contrast to Barbados, its heavily wooded coastal slopes rising to the cloud-shrouded mountains of the hinterland. The back areas of Fort de France adjoining the docks were incredibly shabby, a conglomeration of shanty buildings inter-spaced with the occasional crumbling stone façade covered in peeling posters dating back years. Traffic thronged the streets, driven with typical French aggression on throttle and brake. As Glenn was moved to remark, the sight of a whole line of it setting off from the lights in one solid mass was enough to put the fear of God into any ordinary motorist.

Alex enjoyed the atmosphere of the local street market they discovered close to the river, wandering happily through the colourful disarray of paw-paws and mangoes and green bananas spread in heaps over the cracked concrete of the pavements and watched over by vendors who squatted comfortably in the dust behind each pile. Good-natured raillery greeted them on all sides, although there was little pressure to buy. Apparently cruise ship passengers rarely found their way down this end of the town.

Later on in the afternoon they took a taxi into the town proper to shop along the Rue Victor Hugo for duty-free goods, stopping off at one of the larger hotels to watch a performance by the Ballet Martinique. It was said that the dances, each of which had its own meaning, had been adapted by slaves from those of their French masters and put to the rhythms of their own Beguine music. Alex was able to recognise at least some of the movements from a minuet worked into a dance portraying courtship, and felt her own body itching to move to the tantalising rhythm. It was easy to understand how Cole Porter had found the inspiration for his 'Begin the Beguine' by just listening to the music of the island.

Carnival Night was the big event of the week on board the *Andromeda*, with everyone entering into the spirit of the occasion from dinnertime onwards. Even the restaurant waiters had changed from their normal red and grey jackets to Spanish-style tight black trousers and bright boleros worn over full-sleeved shirts, and there was prolonged applause when the lights were dimmed for two long lines of them to enter bearing the speciality dessert flaming on silver platters.

There was time for an after-dinner drink with Glenn and Sally before it was time for Alex to go and change for her appearance. She reached her dressing room to find Marian Lee already there before her making up her face at the dressing table.

'Guess nobody told you we shared tonight to make room for all the extras,' said the latter, eyeing her cynically through the mirror as she hesitated in the doorway. 'I'll be through in a couple of minutes, and then it's all yours. Why not come in and park yourself while you wait?'

Alex did so, perching uncomfortably on the edge of the spare chair with a feeling that she was the intruder here. Knowing the reason for the antagonism which fairly bristled in the air made it no easier to find a suitable approach, yet she could hardly sit in silence while the other girl finished what she was doing.

At length she said tentatively, 'I saw you dance the other night. You're very good.'

'Thanks.' The one word with heavy irony.

Alex sighed and took the bull fairly and squarely by the horns. 'Look, I know how you must feel over that solo spot. . . . I'd feel the same myself. Only I had nothing to do with it. The Cruise Director made the decision.'

'Sure he did.' Marian didn't bother to turn her head. 'Like he said, the star has to be given priority. I'd do the same in your shoes, only don't expect me to see it that way from this side of the fence. You got what you wanted, so enjoy it while you can.' Her tone altered a fraction. 'You should thank your lucky stars that Clay isn't the type to let personal feelings interfere with his job.'

Alex went very still. 'What does that mean?'

'You know well enough what it means.' This time the redhead did swing her way, a hint of malice in the boldly outlined features. 'I'm talking about you messing up his sister's marriage. He thinks the world of that girl ... perhaps a bit too much, but that's beside the point. Any other man might have found some means of cutting you down to size professionally, the way it hurts, but Clay being Clay he puts the paying customers first, even when it comes to having to play up to someone like you to do it.'

Only Clay could have told Marian all this, Alex reflected, and that had to mean that the dancer was something more to him than just another member of the cabaret. The thought of being discussed by the two of them was hateful, and yet considering that she had made no attempt to straighten Clay out with regard to her true position in the affair she could hardly blame him for accepting her guilt without question. Yet would he really have been prepared to give her the benefit of the doubt if she had told him of her ignorance regarding Ian's marriage? It seemed doubtful. His mind had been made up about her long before they had met, and it was going to take more than her word to convince him now. What she needed was for Ian to clear her, but no doubt he had other matters on his mind right now. In any case, he was hardly to know that she was here on board the *Andromeda* along with his brother-in-law. The only way he was likely to find out was if Clay elected to pass on the information to his sister, in which case he would almost certainly put the former in the picture—wouldn't he?

'Good for him,' she said without altering her expression. 'That's a very professional attitude. You might tell him I said so.'

What reaction the other had been expecting wasn't clear, but Alex's seemingly calm acceptance of the taunts appeared to throw Marian more than a little. She gave her a long, thoughtful look before turning back to finish making up her face, leaving the cabin some few moments later without having spoken again. Alex hated this kind of atmosphere, but could think of no way of getting round it. Marian was determined to blame her for the change in the programme, and nothing she could say or do was going to make any difference. What she could not afford to do was to let any of it prey on her mind before a performance. Personal problems had to become part of another existence once she was out there on the floor.

Glenn and Sally were waiting for her in the Connaught Lounge when she went through after the show. The latter was full of admiration.

'You were terrific,' she exclaimed. 'Why don't you cut some discs, then I'd be able to tell all my friends to buy them.'

Alex laughed. 'I've never been approached to do any recording. I don't think my name is well enough known.'

'It's only a matter of time.' Glenn said it with confidence. 'We've been invited to a party in the Cruise Director's cabin, if you're feeling up to it. Just a small affair for a selected few, I gather.' He sounded amused. 'I'm not sure I merit the distinction, but far be it from me to throw opportunity away. Sally's keen to go.'

Alex's first reaction had been to refuse, but to do so

would probably mean that the Freemans wouldn't go either, she realised. 'Are you quite sure I was included in the invitation?' she asked, and saw Glenn's brows lift in surprise.

'Of course. The steward who brought the message obviously knew we were waiting for you here because he said when Miss Gaynor came offstage would we make our way to Carillon Deck, cabin six-forty.'

Alex met Sally's eyes and came to a quick decision. 'It sounds the next thing to a Royal command,' she said lightly. 'In which case we'd better obey the summons.'

Carillon was her own deck, containing the shopping arcade as well as the Cruise Office. Cabin six-forty was directly opposite this latter, standing alone between two doors marked 'Private'. Alex was surprised to see the size of the place when they were admitted. It was only after a moment or two that she noted the absence of either beds or berths among the fittings and came to the conclusion that it was in all probability a special kept solely for the smaller, more intimate functions of this nature.

Apart from themselves there were perhaps fifteen people in the cabin, spread comfortably around the various chairs and couches, or in one or two cases standing with glasses in hand. Clay Anderson pressed his way through the sea of knees and feet to greet them, his eyes meeting Alex's with an enigmatic expression in their grey depths.

'Glad you could make it,' he said to Glenn, and gave Sally a smile which brought sudden unexpected flags of colour to her cheeks. 'There's a young man over there who thinks he knows you from High School. Come and say Hallo to him.'

Somehow Alex found herself parted from Glenn and sitting between one of the other officers and a Venezuelan passenger who lost little time in telling her admiringly how much he enjoyed her singing. He was more than twice the age of the young Lothario she had encountered the other night, but scarcely more subtle in his attentions. After having had her knee squeezed for the third time in as many minutes, Alex began to look round for some excuse to escape, but Glenn was deep in conversation with a woman on the far side of the cabin, and she could think of no adequate reason why she should suddenly get up and join any of the other groups. Sally was laughing at something being said to her by the tall, athletic-looking young man Clay had indicated. Alex cast a surreptitious glance around for the latter, and found him suddenly in front of her, leaning down to her neighbour to excuse his interruption at the same time as he was drawing her to her feet.

'You don't seem able to cope very well with our South American cousins,' he murmured. 'Let me find you a nice safe Englishman ... one of the few we have aboard.'

He gave her no time to reply, pausing in front of a couple in evening dress who seemed to stand a little apart from the rest, and performing introductions with a perfectly straight face before leaving Alex to face the glassy politeness adopted by such of the British upper crust when addressing the lower orders, among whom paid entertainers apparently ranked. Class snobbery had always amused rather than upset her, and tonight was no exception, especially considering the total American disregard for any such demarcation lines. That Clay had done this purposely needed no underlining, but at least she could deny him the satisfaction of letting him see any discomfiture on her part.

It was Philip who eventually rescued her from tedium, carrying her off to the far side of the room on the pretext of introducing her to some new people.

'Thanks,' she said gratefully. 'It was getting a bit difficult.'

'Can't think why they chose the *Andromeda*,' he said, low-toned. 'They should stick to the *Queen* ... first class, of course.' He got her another Martini, eyeing her smilingly as he handed over the glass. 'You'll have been on board a whole week come tomorrow. How does it feel?'

'I'm finding my feet. Or should I say my legs, in the circumstances? There's still a lot I've got to see, though, both ashore and on board.'

Philip looked down at his own glass. 'I was off duty yesterday when we were in Martinique. I looked for you, but you'd gone ashore with your American friend. He's a widower, isn't he?'

'Yes.' Alex saw no reason to enlarge on that simple statement of fact. Philip was as transparent as daylight in his motives: all he was looking for was her assurance that Glenn meant nothing to her beyond a holiday acquaintanceship. She wondered briefly if it was her own fault that he had managed to develop such an over-riding possessiveness towards her in such a short time, but could think of nothing she had said or done which could have been misconstrued as encouragement.

Half of the draw was, she knew, in the apparent glamour of her job. To the average layman the whole entertainment world glittered like a star. Few, if any, realised the amount of work which went into creating a worthwhile act, or fully appreciated the fact that it *was* a job, just like any other. They only saw the end product, the culmination of days or even weeks of going over and over the same material until it both felt *and* sounded right. The only time glamour in any shape or form even came into it was the few moments when she stood out there under the spotlights wearing a glittering dress and gave her all to that sea of nameless white faces: then and then only did she become the creature of Philip's imagination. Only it was quite useless trying to put all that across to him; he must learn for himself that the singer was only the user of the song.

It was a relief to have Glenn choose that moment to seek her out. She turned her face warmly towards him, conscious of the security of that hand under her arm and shying away from the recollection that by this time tomorrow he would be many miles away. In that same moment she felt Philip withdraw a shade, although he made no actual move. When she looked forward again it was to find Clay viewing the three of them with unconcealed cynicism.

This time she did raise her glass to him, only a fraction, it was true, but enough to make her meaning clear. She had the satisfaction of seeing his lips thin before he refocused his attention on the people he was with at present—except that it somehow wasn't at all satisfying to know she had scored a point off him. The whole business was ridiculous. Why didn't she simply tell him the truth of her association with Ian whether he believed her or not? It shouldn't be of any concern to her *what* he believed, if it came to that, but she knew that it was. Clay Anderson was not a man towards whom one could feel indifferent. Alex only wished that he was.

The party broke up at one. Offered a formal farewell by Clay, Alex was content to let Glenn make the necessary expressions of appreciation for the occasion. There was no sign of Sally when they reached the foyer again. Nor could Alex spot the young American with whom she had spent the greater part of the last couple of hours.

'They've gone up to Beach Deck for a last look at the Caribbean by moonlight,' Glenn informed her, sensing her question. 'She'll come to no harm with young Craig. It turns out that I have business connections with his father. A pity we didn't run into them before this. It's amazing how you can go a whole week on a ship this size without once coming across folk.' He paused. 'I thought we might take a last stroll along the Boat Deck ourselves? It will probably be the last time I have you to myself before we board the plane home tomorrow.'

And when Glenn was gone, what then? For the first time Alex acknowledged that she had been using him this last week as a guard against Clay, and after to-morrow she would have no protection.

'That would be nice,' she heard herself saying.

At this hour the open decks were almost deserted, although the Calypso Club was still going strong, judging from the strains of music which managed to filter down this far. The two of them paced slowly for'ard until they reached the board which said 'Crew Only', stopping there to lean companionably side by side on the rail and gaze out over the slow rolling blackness.

'No moon tonight,' Glenn observed in conversational tones, and Alex smiled.

'There's a song in there somewhere. Sally and her new friend are going to be disappointed.'

'They're not on their own.' He looked down at her for a long moment before turning her gently round to face him. His face was serious. 'I'm going to miss you, Alex. These last few days have been ... Well, if I'm any closer to Sally now it's due entirely to you. She's grown very fond of you.'

'And I of her.' She was relaxed in his grasp, trusting him as she would have trusted few others. 'You've made my first week a great deal easier between you.'

His smile was a trifle wry. 'I'd hoped there might have been a little more to it than that. I've found myself able to talk to you as I've been able to talk to few women since Sally's mother died. Oh, there have been other women in my life ... I didn't mean I'd been entirely celibate ... but there's a world of difference between them and you. Despite the gap in our ages I feel on the same wavelength with you. Or is that assuming too much?'

Alex shook her head. 'I don't think so. I've always felt more at ease with older men, perhaps for that very reason.' She paused briefly, knowing what he was building up to and suddenly not caring. 'I'll miss you too, Glenn.'

His kiss was gentle, undemanding and yet somehow like a pact between them. Alex felt no thrill of excitement at his touch, only a warming sense of being needed. Glenn might be old enough to be her father when it came to actual years, but that in no way detracted from his inner youth. He reminded her of Barney, and she could pay no man any greater compliment than that.

'We're going to keep in touch,' he said softly when he released her. 'I'd like to come over when you go back home and renew our ... friendship.'

'I'll look forward to it.' Alex said it with sincerity, conscious of the three long months stretching between.

She made no attempt to pursue the quivering sensation deep down within her at the thought of those same three months right here on board the *Andromeda*.

They docked in San Juan at eight o'clock. Alex was early on deck to view procedure under the hot morning sun, seeing the colour-washed harbour buildings with a feeling that weeks rather than mere days had passed since she had last been there. The Freemans' flight was not until the afternoon. Alex was to spend the morning with them sightseeing in the town, and then lunch before seeing them into a taxi for the airport. Then it would be back to the ship for her, with a whole day at sea to face on the morrow.

Glenn and Sally came over to her table after they had finished breakfast to collect her. The Millers were leaving the ship today too. Alex took her leave of them with regret, realising that tonight at dinner there would be strangers in their places. She would grow accustomed to new faces in the course of these next few weeks, but at the moment it seemed just one more cross to bear.

With their luggage already taken ashore ready for transportation directly to the airport, the Freemans had nothing to worry about but themselves and their hand luggage for the next six hours. By common consent they elected to walk into the old part of the town, cutting through the cobbled square which formed part of the waterfront and taking one of the long, steeply climbing streets out of it towards the Atlantic side of the narrow promontory.

It was gaspingly hot within the airless confines of the old, peeling buildings, the kind of heat which sapped the strength and created instant lethargy. Even the two magnificent Borzoi hounds held on leash by a passing man looked as if they found the effort of exercising their muscles a little too much for them, fine heads hanging and tongues lolling out. Alex followed the trio idly with her eyes as they went through a door set into a feature-less cement-rendered wall, and found herself looking through into a courtyard straight out of seventeenth-century Spain, with wrought-iron balconies overhanging a rough paved central floor. Flowers climbed the whitewashed walls and hung in profusion from the rails themselves, while from a central pool a fountain of water sparkled invitingly as it splashed back into the stone basin. The door had closed again before she could draw the attention of the others, leaving her to view the battered wood and dirty yellow wall both in wonder and confusion. Apparently the Puerto Ricans in this part of town believed in keeping any beauty entirely for themselves.

It was different when they came out at the head of the Calle and saw the Atlantic stretching away before them. Up here the air was fresh and tangy, although the sun blazed away unrelentingly. Palm trees shaded graceful cream and white-walled villas overlooking the sea, while across the road ran the wall which still enclosed a good part of the old town after more than three hundred years.

The three of them followed it along to the Fort San Cristobal, passing through the deserted peace of its arched courtyards to the battlements, from where there was a magnificent view of the whole town both old and new. Below, and seemingly almost close enough to reach out and touch, was the *Andromeda*, berthed in line with a whole row of other cruise ships, their white-painted superstructures dazzling to the eye.

'That must be the other fort, El Morro,' said Glenn,

pointing right to where it was possible to see more battlements rising. 'I believe the Spaniards fought your own Francis Drake from there. It was impregnable from the sea, although the British did manage to take it for a brief time from the landward side round about the end of the sixteenth century.'

'Dad, I'm sure Alex doesn't need a history lesson,' protested his daughter, and he looked suddenly and endearingly sheepish.

'Sorry, I guess I got a bit carried away. I was reading up about the place before we docked this morning. Actually, I'd thought the U.S. Army still ran it, but apparently we moved out some time ago.'

Alex was smiling. 'Well, you've told me something I didn't know about our part in it. History was never my best subject at school, particularly when it came to battles over this and that. We seem to have been a very acquisitive lot all through.' Her glance had moved in the opposite direction, following the path of the three-lane highway running parallel with the waterfront towards the thrust of modern tower blocks on the skyline. 'It's like two separate places rather than the one town. This end seems to be the poorer as well as the older. Did you notice how many crippled people there were among those we passed coming up here? I counted five on crutches in the space of five minutes.'

'No, I didn't,' he confessed. 'Perhaps because I didn't want to see them. This is the first time I've visited the older part of San Juan. On the two other occasions I've been down this way it's been on someone else's expense account, and that means you stay where the business is.' He paused before adding evenly, 'My grandfather was born in the Bowery, but he still managed to have his own business before he was thirty.'

Alex looked at him. 'You're saying that poverty is just a state of mind?'

'The acceptance of it is. I could go down there and give one of those people five hundred dollars and within a month they'd be back where they started. Folk like that live for now, not for the future. It wouldn't occur to them to spend only enough of that five hundred to fill their stomachs and make the rest work for them.'

Maybe because no one ever took the trouble to tell them how, Alex reflected, but she didn't say it. It would be a shame to spoil their last day together arguing an issue neither of them could do a great deal about.

They took a taxi into the main town and shopped for last-minute gifts along the beautiful wide thoroughfares, lunched at the Da Vinci and lingered over coffee until it was time for the Freemans to take their leave. Sally had tears in her eyes as she hugged Alex goodbye on the kerbside before stepping into the car which was to take them to the airport.

'I hope we'll see you again some time,' she said. 'It would be wonderful if you came over to the States to work. You would let us know, wouldn't you?'

Alex promised that she would, and kept the smile fixed on her face as Glenn walked her back to the second car waiting to take her to the ship. Only then did he press into her hands the small package he had carried with him from the hotel.

'I want you to have this as a memento of the time we spent together,' he said gruffly. 'I bought it in Martinique while you and Sally were looking at those Swiss watches. It goes with your eyes.' His hand closed over her fingers, making her hold on to the package as she made to protest. 'Please don't say no, Alex. It means a lot to me to think that you have something I gave you.

It's only a small thing, but it comes with my deepest regards.'

Alex protested no more. It would have seemed churlish in the circumstances to have done so. 'Thank you,' she said softly. 'I just wish I had something to give you in return.'

'You already did that.' He made no move to kiss her, perhaps conscious of Sally's proximity in the other cab, simply taking her free hand in his and squeezing it before helping her into her seat.

The last glimpse Alex had of him was a tall distinguished figure on the pavement edge as her cab turned the corner.

She waited until she was in her cabin before opening the present, taking off the wrappings to reveal the small, leather-bound jeweller's box with a feeling that Glenn's idea of something small might not coincide with her own. If it did it was certainly only in the actual size of the pendant occupying the box. It was made of beaten figured silver shaped like a flower, with a single green stone forming the centre. Not a real emerald, of course, but Alex knew that even so the piece must have cost a great deal of money. It put her in a dilemma. Some small, inexpensive trifle she would have accepted without any qualms, but this was different. No matter how much Glenn had enjoyed her company she had done nothing to merit such a gift from him. It was too much!

And yet, common sense asserted, it was probably only her own sense of values which saw it that way. To someone like Glenn Freeman price was of no importance; he had chosen the piece simply because it matched the colour of her eyes. She looked at it for a long moment before finally taking it from the box to hold it against the bare, already bronzed skin of her throat, seeing the light catch and sparkle the stone. It certainly was a lovely thing, yet it still didn't feel right to accept such an obviously expensive piece of costume jewellery from a man she had known less than a week. On the other hand, how would he feel if she returned it to him by post after he had gone to the trouble of buying it especially for her in the first place? She doubted if she could make him understand the way she felt; she wasn't all that sure she understood herself.

Eventually she accepted that she was going to have to keep it, and resolved to write to Glenn right there and then expressing her gratitude. If she put the letter in the box here on board before six it would be taken off with the evening collection and posted directly from San Juan. By airmail he should receive it within a couple of days. Meanwhile, if she was keeping it she might as well wear it. It would go beautifully with her white dress.

She was halfway through writing the letter when a tap on the door heralded the entry of the steward with a message requesting her company at the Cruise Director's table that same evening. On the point of refusing, Alex paused, realising just how Clay would take any reluctance on her part to be in his company. It wasn't as though they would be alone at the table; he always had a gathering of at least four people. Providing Marian Lee was not among them tonight Alex thought she could bear the strain. Better that than having Clay believe her afraid of him.

She took particular care in dressing for dinner later on. The white dress was one of her favourites, sleeveless and cut to a deep V both back and front. The pendant nestled just below the hollow of her throat, its stone catching the light in a way which aroused a faint stirring of unease again before she resolutely turned her thoughts away from the direction in which they were leading. She had taken up her hair into a smooth chignon, with two long tendrils escaping to curl softly over her ears, emphasising her eyes with a smudge of violet shadow. Her face in the mirror looked calm and composed. No one looking at her could possibly guess the true state of her nerves. She felt as strung up as a piano wire, and all at the thought of seeing Clay again. Dislike him as a person she might, but there was no denying the effect he had on her senses.

He was waiting at his table when she reached the restaurant, and he was alone. He rose as she approached and pulled out the chair on his right-hand side, standing there with his hand on the back and an odd little smile on his lips.

'You're causing quite a sensation among our new passengers,' he commented. 'Good advance work!'

Alex bit her lip as she took her seat. Trust him to think she had only got herself up this way to promote her image! Still, better that he should believe that than imagine *he* might be the one she was trying to impress.

'Maybe I could have a fanfare of trumpets next time,' she quipped. 'Am I early or are your other guests late?'

'Neither. You and I are dining alone.' He took his own seat, having settled her in hers, meeting her eyes across the space between the two of them with arrogant assurance. 'There's no one among the new consignment I felt it necessary to honour on the first night, so for once I'm indulging my own requirements.'

Alex stiffened imperceptibly. 'I wouldn't have said we had enough in common to carry us through without strain.'

'No?' He moved his gaze deliberately down from her

eyes to her mouth, lingering there for a brief moment before coming to rest at the base of her throat where Glenn's pendant nestled so beautifully. The grey eyes narrowed suddenly. 'You haven't worn that before.'

'It was a present.' Involuntarily her hand went up to touch the piece as if in reassurance as she saw the hardness come into his face. 'It's rather pretty, don't you think?'

His laugh was harsh. 'Oh yes, it's that all right! I suppose Freeman gave it to you.'

'As a matter of fact he did. This afternoon just before he left for the airport. I suppose you think I shouldn't have accepted it.'

'Not at all,' with irony. 'A woman would be a fool to turn down an emerald in any circumstances.'

Alex stared at him, her breath sharp-edged in her throat. 'It isn't real.'

He put out a hand and slid it under the pendant, the backs of his fingers resting against her skin as he studied it. 'It's real,' he stated with enough certainty to convince her. 'Not an enormous stone maybe, but worth about twelve hundred dollars in that setting. Congratulations.'

Anger flashed in her eyes, momentarily overriding all other reactions. 'All right, so I'm a naïve idiot, but I didn't realise. If I'd known of course I'd never have accepted it!'

Her vehemence gave him pause, although the line of his mouth did not relax. He studied her for a moment, then shrugged. 'True or not, you've got the thing, and as Freeman is by this time back in the States it's a bit late to start protesting. You'll just have to accept your good fortune.'

'I can't. I shall have to send it back.' She reached up

to the clasp with fingers that trembled. 'I'll take it off before anything happens to it.'

'Don't be ridiculous. Leave it where it is. It's probably safer there than in your purse.' His expression had lost nothing of its cynicism. 'Look, it isn't any of my concern what presents you're given. If Freeman thinks enough of you to give you an emerald ... and I can imagine he can well afford it ... then why look a gift horse in the mouth? No doubt you'll be able to thank him properly some time.'

Alex thought numbly of the letter already on its way doing just that, realising that in writing it she had to all intents and purposes acknowledged full approval of the gift. There was nothing in the letter to lead Glenn to suppose that she had not appreciated the full value of the pendant, and he almost certainly was not the kind of man who gave away emeralds to every woman he met—at least, not after just a few days. By accepting it she had laid herself open to misinterpretation in more ways than one, and at the moment she could see no way out of it without hurting a man she regarded with both respect and affection.

The waiter arrived to take their order just then. By the time they were alone again Alex was sufficiently in command of herself to come to one definite decision.

'I'd like to have this put in safe keeping after we've eaten,' she said. 'Can it be arranged?'

'There's a safe in the Purser's office for passengers' valuables.' He was looking at her rather oddly. 'You know, I can't quite make you out. You're not consistent.'

Something hardened inside her. 'With what? Your image of what I should be? Maybe I just don't care for emeralds. They're supposed to be unlucky, aren't they?'

'So they say.' His own attitude had hardened again to match. 'Forget it.'

If there had been any opening at all for better understanding between them it was past and gone now. They were back where they had started, wary and contemptuous. And that, Alex resolved, was how it could stay. She had had enough of Clay Anderson to last her a lifetime.

CHAPTER FOUR

ALEX spent most of Sunday trying to compose another letter to Glenn, only to tear up each successive effort in despairing acknowledgement of her inability to say what she wanted to say in words which would cause no misunderstanding. If she hadn't been quite so quick in sending off the first letter this whole affair would have been relatively simple, but as it was there was nothing she could do but keep on trying and hope that inspiration would eventually come.

She had left Clay as soon as it was decently possible after they had finished dinner the previous night, returning to her cabin to take off the pendant and replace it in its box. As soon as the Purser's office had opened this morning she had taken it along and seen it into the safe with a feeling of relief. At least nothing could happen to it while it was there, giving her a little time to decide what exactly she was going to do about it. Meanwhile, life had to carry on as normal.

At three she joined James Keen and Sol Dayton, the pianist, in the Connaught Room for a run through of one or two fresh songs. In spite of the weekly turnover in clientele, Alex preferred to keep ringing the changes in each night's programme, as much for her own benefit as anyone else's. There was a new American release at present topping the charts both sides of the Atlantic which was perfect for her style. The three of them hammered out an arrangement between them and decided to put it in that same evening. Before closing the session, Alex expressed her grateful thanks to both men for the help they had given her, aware of her good fortune in having such a sympathetic backing. So far as her act was concerned she had no particular worries at all. She could only wish that happy state would extend itself to other areas of her shipboard life.

She waited until most people had already left the ship's side on the Monday morning before disembarking in La Guaira herself. Philip was on duty at the head of the gangway. He greeted her with some faint reservation.

'You're not thinking of wandering around the streets on your own, are you?' he queried with a trace of anxiety. 'Looking the way you do you'd be asking for trouble.'

Alex was wearing linen slacks in a pale pink with a matching shirt opened only at the throat—an outfit she had considered both practical and conservative. She smiled back at Philip from beneath the brim of her floppy white hat and pushed the strap of her raffia bag further up her shoulder in a gesture which unconsciously asserted her ability to look after herself.

'I thought of taking a taxi up to the cableway and

going over into Caracas. I'm told it's a sight not to be missed from the top.'

'Always providing you can see it. There's often a lot of low cloud up there.' He paused. 'You could have gone on the organised tour. They come back that way.'

She pulled a face. 'I don't like being organised. Where's the best place to find a taxi?'

'There's a rank beyond the Terminal.' He obviously saw the uselessness of arguing any further. 'Any of them will take you wherever you want to go, but fix a price with them first or you'll be fleeced.'

'Thanks.' She put a hand on his sleeve in passing. 'Philip, you mustn't worry about me. I'll be fine. I like sightseeing on my own.'

She lingered for rather longer than she had intended in the Terminal building itself, fascinated by the shops selling everything one could imagine. Some cacique gold coins caught her eye; they would look good made up into a bracelet. But they were a little too expensive here so close to the ship. Common sense told her she would obtain them far more reasonably elsewhere in the town.

Coming out into the sunlight again she caught her breath at the sheer magnificence of the mountains climbing away from the coast in ever-increasing height and splendour, cloud-wreathed at their highest points. On the far side of those peaks lay the capital of Caracas, reputedly one of the most beautiful cities in the world. In spite of what she had told Philip back there on the ship she wished she had someone to share it all with.

Shrugging off the sudden sense of desolation, she walked over to the first in the line of long American cars waiting for passengers, trying to ignore the openly speculative stares of the men lounging idly alongside their vehicles. The driver of her chosen transport was sitting in the front reading a newspaper, one elbow resting on the frame of the wound-down window. He glanced up at her approach, dark features visibly lighting up, whether at the prospect of a fare or at her appearance, Alex wasn't certain. He was youngish and swarthily good-looking, with a head of curly black hair. The most important factor, to her, was the small ticket tucked into a corner of the windscreen pronouncing the driver's ability to speak English. What little she knew of the Spanish language would barely have been enough to do any haggling over costs.

'I'd like to go up to the cableway, please,' she said clearly, and saw a broad smile break over the man's face.

'Sure, lady,' he said. He got out of the car to open the rear door for her, looking cool and comfortable if not particularly businesslike in his cotton tee-shirt and slacks. 'It's a good day to go up the mountain.'

'What do you charge?' she asked with her foot already inside the step. 'I mean, is there a fixed rate for the journey?'

Once again the smile, accompanied by a shake of the head. 'No fixed rate. We reach an agreement when we get there. Pedro won't take you for a ride, lady.'

Alex had to laugh. There was something reassuring in his very ease of manner. 'I'll believe you.'

He closed all the windows before starting the engine, switching on the air-conditioning as he turned the vehicle in a tight sweep to head down the length of the broad jetty towards the road proper. Alex had opened her mouth to protest instinctively against the idea of travelling in a closed car, but closed it again when she felt the delicious coolness of the air over her damp skin. There would be plenty of time to take in the Venezuelan climate later.

La Guaira was a small compact town of colonial-style buildings scattered here and there with modern blocks of shops and offices, the foothills at its rear covered from base to summit in a higgledy-piggledy mess of shanty dwellings which even from a distance seemed ready to fall down about the owners' ears.

'That's where the common people live,' Pedro commented, catching the direction of her interest through the driving mirror. 'The poorer they are the higher up they live. The Government built flats for these people, but they can't afford to pay the rent, so the flats stand empty still. It's one of those things, as you would say in your part of the world.'

Alex thought it time to change the subject. 'Where did you learn to speak English so well?'

'From the Americans,' with a humorous intonation. 'The tourists come all the year round to La Guaira. We don't have very many English.'

Alex could imagine. 'This is my first visit to South America,' she acknowledged. 'I only wish there was more time to see something of it. It's impossible to get any real impression in one day.'

'To do that you have to live in a place, lady. You'll like Caracas. All the tourists like Caracas.'

'I'm sure they do.' Alex realised it was little use trying to convince this Venezuelan cynic of any real interest in his country on her part. To him she was just another sightseer, one of the privileged class able to travel the world without having to count the cost. It seemed pointless to mention that she was actually employed on board the *Andromeda* herself.

The cableway terminal was housed beneath an enormous arched roof extending down to low concrete pillars which allowed in air but kept out the rays of the sun. Pedro went and bought her a ticket himself from the kiosk, returning to where she stood a little apart from the general throng waiting to climb aboard one of the bright yellow cars.

'You go up there and take the other car down when you're ready,' he said. 'I meet you on the other side and take you round Caracas, then bring you back to the ship through the mountain pass. This way you see everything.'

It certainly sounded a better idea than taking her chances of finding other transport when she did reach the capital, and it obviously wasn't the first time Pedro had suggested an extension of his hire. What it was all going to cost she daren't begin to imagine, but what did it really matter for once? She was earning enough to indulge herself.

'Supposing I decide not to come down the other side after all?' she suggested with a tilt of her lips. 'For all you know I might seize the opportunity to get out of paying you anything at all!'

His grin was quick and easy. 'Lady, if I thought that I wouldn't be making the offer. It's half an hour to the top. Most people spend an hour or so up there, so in two hours from now I'll be waiting at the Caracas Terminal.'

Somehow Alex found herself ahead of the queue and seated in the first car. Pedro lifted a hand in farewell as the cables began to hum, then turned and strode casually out into the sunshine again to where he had left his own car. Alex gripped the rail in front of her, gazing straight ahead through the glass which formed the rear side of the cage and feeling her stomach lurch as they lifted out of the dimness into brilliant light in a steep climb up the mountainside.

Soon the terminal was just a splodge of concrete hundreds of feet below, while before her and to either hand stretched an ever-widening panorama of blue sea and sparkling coastline. Around her rose the mountain, green and lush, traversed by narrow white paths which meandered with apparent aimlessness round every crag and cranny. Here and there were dotted little white dwellings which clung to the slopes like mountain goats, hovering protectively above terraced fields of crops.

Further up still and they began to glide over forests of pine, with the high crags looming above and beyond like sentinels at a gate. The car slid over a ridge and the coastline vanished, so that the mountains themselves seemed to rise straight out of the sea. There was a tang in the air which tickled the nostrils, a clarity which stood every spur of rock in sharp relief against the sky-line. Alex was lost in a haze of delight, the other occupants of the car totally forgotten as she soaked up the beauty all round her. This, she knew, was an experience she would never forget.

Reaching the top was almost an anti-climax. Impatient to see the view from these heights, she did not linger within the glass-sided terminal with its gift shop and café, but followed the signs along a ramp to exit on to a paved pathway leading along the top of the mountain towards a towering structure pointing like a finger at the heavens. There was another, smaller cable-way running parallel to the path and about thirty feet above it, but the gondolas were motionless and rusting, the cables slack. Alex recalled Glenn mentioning something about a hotel built up here as a tourist draw, only to be closed down again within months owing to the frequency with which the cloud obscured the view. Someone must have lost a fortune on such an ambitious project, and all because of a lack of forethought. Alex could only be grateful that today the atmosphere was clear.

The place was locked and already semi-derelict. She peered in through glass doors at the mouldering mosaic and huge windows of what had once been a magnificent foyer, wondering what would eventually be done with what must be one of the world's largest white elephants. In front of the main building extended a circular paved area containing several bench seats and a couple of flowerbeds running riot. Alex followed a small group of Americans to the low stone wall surrounding the perimeter of the courtyard and saw the city of Caracas spread out far below in glittering splendour—a lost world among the all-encompassing mountains.

Cloud drifted in cottonwool patches a few hundred feet below where she stood, lending light and shade to the valley floor. Even from this height one could pick out the individual streets and thoroughfares, the parks and squares; catch the ant-like movement of traffic. It was almost impossible to imagine that in less than an hour she would be down there herself, traversing those same streets, seeing those same sights from a totally different perspective.

Back at the Terminal she bought postcards and stamps and scribbled off a couple of hasty messages to friends back home, slipping them into the box provided. Another car load from La Guaira came laughing and exclaiming through from the disembarkation point, splitting into individual groups, each intent upon a particular pursuit.

Alex made her way through to the Caracas station, this time with orange cars as opposed to the yellow of the other side. The wide platforms were crowded, mostly with schoolchildren being urged along by a couple of harassed-looking teachers whose task Alex did not envy. Trying to find the spot at which the queue proper began, she found herself caught up and swept along inexorably with the tide of eager youngsters already clambering into the waiting car. A hand lightly caught her elbow as she stumbled over the sill, guiding her to a seat, then there came the sound of the sliding doors closing and the sudden lurch of movement. Alex turned to thank the man who had slid into the seat alongside her, and felt the words die on her lips as she met the familiar mocking grey gaze.

'It looks as though we're stuck with one another for twenty minutes or so,' Clay said. 'One of the hazards of getting mixed up with a school party. I gather you came from La Guaira alone?'

'Yes.' Alex gathered her scattered wits about her, a dozen questions darting through her mind at once. In the casual shirt and denim slacks he hardly seemed the same fellow, yet there was little difference in the quality of his regard. 'How did you ... I mean, I didn't see you back here in the Terminal.'

'No?' He shrugged. 'I was with one or two others from the ship, but I'm afraid they got left behind. They'll probably get in the next car.'

Meanwhile she had his company to bear, like it or not, Alex reflected. Well, after Saturday's episode she was making no effort towards camaraderie of any kind. She had come up here to see the scenery. As it was, a great deal of her pleasure in that was already ruined by Clay's presence.

It proved quite impossible, however, to stop any small exclamations of admiration and delight as the city came slowly closer. Nor could she fail to appreciate Clay's familiarity with the scene as he pointed out landmarks.

'That over there is La Rinconada, the race track,' he said, indicating a great open area over on the right. 'There's no other to equal it. No racing today, but it's always open for inspection. You'll need a taxi to take you out there, though.'

'I have one,' she told him. 'The man who brought me out from the town will be waiting for me when I get down. Or so he said.'

'Oh, he'll be there. It's common practice. Means a full day's hire as opposed to a few bitty little jobs. Did you settle a price with him first?'

'No, I didn't. He said he wouldn't overcharge me.'

'Depends what *he* calls overcharging. Women don't normally tour out here on their own. He might be tempted to take advantage.' She stole a glance at him, to meet a sardonic glance back. 'Both ways, if you're not careful.'

Her mouth compressed. 'I don't see why it should concern you if I get rooked.'

'You happen to be off the *Andromeda* and that makes you my responsibility. I'd better have a word or two with this driver when we get down.'

'I'll handle it myself, thanks.'

'No, you won't.' The statement was quiet but held a note which brooked no argument.

They spent the rest of the descent in silence, but Alex could no longer concentrate on the view. Short of hiding from Clay when she got to the bottom she could

see no way out of this situation. She bitterly resented
his interference even while having to acknowledge a
certain sense in what he said. If Pedro demanded a hundred dollars for his day's work she had no way of knowing whether that was extortionate or merely the normal
rate for the job.

She could see the Venezuelan waiting at the turnstile
even as they descended from the car amidst the chattering crowd of youngsters. Clay paced purposefully at her
side towards the exit, passing through to confront the
taxi-driver with an appraising eye.

'You're taking this lady on from here?'

Alex caught Pedro's quick glance and lifted her
shoulders in a manner meant to deny all responsibility
for the intrusion. Embarrassed, she pretended an interest in her immediate surroundings as the two men
talked, trying not to listen to the conversation. A crowd
of passengers for the cableway came towards the turnstile, forcing her to step backwards out of the way.
When they had gone she saw Clay turning back to her.

'It's settled,' he said. 'Thirty dollars for the whole
hire, plus any tip we think the tour is worth.'

Her heart jerked. 'We?'

'I'm coming with you.' His tone defied her to argue
with *that*. 'Downtown first, I think, to La Rinconada,
and then a quick lunch before we take in the rest.'

She stared at him, aware of the involuntary curl of
anticipation deep inside her. Regardless of what her
mind said her senses refused to recognise him as anything but a vitally attractive man. He wasn't the one
she feared as much as herself, she admitted in fleeting
self-analysis.

'Aren't you taking rather a lot for granted?' she

asked, refusing to give in without any struggle at all. 'I suppose it didn't occur to you that I might prefer to be alone.'

'It occurred to me. It certainly couldn't have been for lack of willing companions.' His expression didn't alter. 'I'm still coming with you, so if you want to see Caracas I'd suggest you make the best of it.' There was a pause and a slight change of tone. 'We might both try forgetting a few things just for today.'

'A truce, you mean?'

'Something like that.'

'All right.' She took the olive branch for what it appeared to be, pushing suspicion to the back of her mind. Perhaps Clay was going to give her a chance to tell her side of the story at last. If only she could make him understand, or at least give her the benefit of the doubt. If only they could become friends instead of enemies. She let her thoughts stray no further than that. It would be enough just to stop fighting him.

Pedro appeared to have accepted the whole business philosophically, although Alex was aware of his speculative gaze through the driving mirror as she settled herself in the rear seat again. What he must be thinking of Clay's intervention she had no idea and didn't particularly care to know. She felt the slight pressure of a broad shoulder as the latter eased himself alongside her, and had to stop herself moving away to the far corner of the seat to avoid any further contact. He was too astute not to have guessed why she found it necessary to move away from him. He had enough of an advantage over her without giving him more.

'What about your friends?' she asked as they began to move off. 'Won't they wonder where you got to?'

'They'll assume I took off on my own.' He sounded unconcerned.

The journey out to the race track did not take long. Alex was enthralled by the beauty of the city, by the symmetry of design and sympathetic mingling of old and new. All around, in whichever direction one looked, rose the mountains, shading from green to brown to purple, a seemingly impenetrable barrier against the outside world.

La Rinconada was an experience in itself, from the tree-shaded gardens at its front to the superb view across the city afforded from its stands. The centre of the track was laid out in an ornamental garden complete with lakes and waterfalls, while each of the three stands boasted its own restaurant and bar, plus a closed-circuit television system for those who preferred to watch the racing from the comfort of a table or bar stool.

In addition to all this, Clay told her, the track possessed a breeding centre and hospital second to none.

Despite her admiration for the architecture of the course, Alex could not help recalling the shanty dwellers Pedro had spoken of. Millions of bolivars must have been spent to make La Rinconada what it was. Surely some of that could have been put to better use.

'Well over two hundred million,' Clay agreed when she put the question to him. And then catching her drift, 'But as a business it provides jobs for more than twenty thousand Venezuelan families as well as contributing most of its profits to the National Treasury. Every country has its poor. It's part of the social structure.'

'You sound like Glenn,' she murmured without

thinking, and felt him glance at her. 'How is it you know so much about this place?' she tagged on hurriedly.

'Interest.' If she had imagined she might be let off the hook she had been mistaken. 'Are you corresponding with the Freemans?'

'They asked me to.' Alex made a point of emphasising the 'they'. She paused, then on impulse added, 'I'm still trying to decide what to do about that pendant. I must return it, of course, but I don't want to hurt Glenn's feelings more than I can help.'

It was a moment or two before he answered, and when he did it was in measured tones. 'Only one person can sort it out, and that's yourself.'

'I wasn't asking for advice,' she retorted, stung. 'You still don't believe I didn't realise it was a genuine emerald, do you?'

He lifted his shoulders. 'I've told you, where you're concerned I'm not sure what to believe. If it weren't for what I know ...' He broke off, his jaw taking on a harder line. 'I thought we'd agreed to forget all that for today.'

'So we did.' She didn't want to forget it; she wanted to plunge right in and explain the situation between her and Ian as it had actually happened, but some stronger instinct drove her to deny that need. 'I think I've seen all I want to see here. Can we move on?'

Pedro had waited in the car. He straightened in his seat as they came out through the 'A' stand turnstile, and switched on the engine.

'Where next?' he asked laconically, and Alex noted that it was Clay he was addressing, not both of them.

'Calle Medio,' he was told. 'About halfway along there's a place called Blanco's.'

'I know it.' There was a new quality of appreciation in the Venezuelan's swift acknowledgement. 'You're with the ships?'

'Right.' Clay consulted his watch. 'You'd better take the long way round. We're not going to have much time for sightseeing after we've eaten.'

They went back through the very heart of the city via tree-lined boulevards twice the width of any normal city roadway, spending half an hour in the old cathedral and marvelling at the splendour of the gold-domed capital building. A little further along they stopped again to view the National Pantheon, burial place of the country's heroes. One enterprising souvenir seller wielded a Polaroid camera and offered to take them together in front of the impressive monument. About to refuse, Alex saw Clay nod permission and felt his arm come about her shoulders, drawing her in to his side. Looking at the developed print some two minutes later she noted the mocking tilt of his lips without surprise.

'You ordered it, *you* have it,' she retorted when he offered the print to her. 'You could pin it up and use it for darts practice, if nothing else.'

The strong mouth widened briefly. 'Let's go and eat.'

Blanco's turned out to be one of those small, outwardly shabby little restaurants which never reach the brochures. The walls were hung with woven Indian rugs, they in turn festooned with bows and arrows and handmade shopping bags which appeared to be for sale along with the food.

The latter was all that Alex had been led to anticipate by Pedro's reaction to the name. For a main course they had a local speciality called *hallacas,* made from cornmeal with meat and vegetables and spices, all wrapped in banana leaves and cooked in water. For dessert she could only manage a little fresh pineapple, sitting back at the end of it with a sigh of content.

'That was delicious. I'm afraid I ate far too much!'

'You can afford it.' Clay finished his wine and pressed his chair an inch or two further from the table in order to ease his legs. 'Not the most comfortable place to eat, but one of the few where you can get an *hallacas* like that.'

'Do you always come here?'

'Most weeks. Not often by cableway, though. Most times I hire a car and drive myself round by road. Today was a fortunate exception.'

'Fortunate?'

'For you. Think what you might have missed.'

She met his gaze with cool deliberation. 'You mean the food.'

'What else?' There was a challenge in the grey eyes. 'Left to your own devices you'd probably have plumped for the Hilton. I thought the change might do you good.'

'They say a change is as good as a rest.' Her glance at her watch was instinctive. 'What time do we sail?'

'Not until six. That gives us almost three hours to kill.'

'You told Pedro to be back here at three.'

'Which means there's a chance he'll make it for half past. Still plenty of time to get back to La Guaira. The road journey takes roughly an hour. Would you like a drink?'

Alex started to shake her head, then purposely changed her mind. 'I'll have a brandy.'

'I doubt if Blanco stocks any. Apart from the local plonk he usually only carries rum. Why not try a

Ponche? It's similar to a Planter's Punch with fruit, etcetera. Refreshing.'

It was. Very. It was also highly intoxicating, although Alex failed to realise just how much until she was over halfway down the tall glass, and by then she was in no mood to care overmuch. Smiling, she looked round the dim, noisy little restaurant and then back at Clay.

'I'm glad you brought me here.'

He inclined his head. 'My pleasure.' He paused before adding, 'I'd have thought your tastes ran to something rather more sophisticated even when you're supposedly slumming.'

'Meaning you chose this place as a salutary lesson?'

'In a way. It's still true that the food can't be bettered, but ...'

'But you didn't believe that was the most essential requirement so far as I'm concerned,' she finished for him without bitterness. 'Less than three years ago I wouldn't even have had the courage to walk into the Hilton, much less eat there. If my tastes run to the West End rather than a Bloomsbury Pizza Parlour now it's only because it happens to be closer to where I live and work. And you can eat good food in simple surroundings even there if you know where to go.'

'You live in Kensington, don't you?'

'Yes.' She eyed him uncertainly. 'How did you know?'

'June mentioned it in her letter.' He took a long swallow of his own Ponche, setting the glass down again with a small thud. 'Ian visited you there?'

'Once or twice after a show for supper.' She saw the hardness of his mouth and made a small impulsive gesture of protest. 'Clay, it wasn't like you think, I ... We didn't ...'

'Forget it.' His tone was abrupt. 'I'm not interested in your motives.'

'Then you shouldn't have brought the subject up.' Anger took the edge over hurt. 'You're not averse to discussing your sister's marital problems with everyone, I notice!'

His eyes narrowed. 'Meaning who, for instance?'

'Oh, you've told more than one person?' The sarcasm was bitter-sweet. 'Maybe you should try being a little more selective in your confidants.'

'Who?' He said it through his teeth, his fingers curling around the glass with a force which suggested an urge to put them around her neck.

Alex shrugged. 'Ask your girl-friend.'

'My ...' He broke off, an odd expression passing fleetingly across his face. 'Are you talking about Marian Lee by any chance?'

So it was true. Alex tried to close her mind against the small shaft which momentarily pierced her. This man's love life meant nothing to her, it *couldn't* mean anything to her!

'If I am it isn't by chance. I'm not sure just what you did tell her ...'

'I told her nothing. The only person I've ever mentioned it to is you. If Marian knows about you and Ian she must have heard us discussing it.'

Alex said with irony, 'Is that what you call it? When, for instance?'

'It could have been your first night on board. I bumped into her just inside the Calypso Club door after you left. She could quite well have been on deck when we were talking. Sound carries at night.'

'A pity you didn't think of that when you started

discussing the subject out there in the first place. Do all your women act that way?'

His eyes were cold. 'Not twice. What exactly did she say to you?'

'You'd better ask her that.'

'I'm asking you!'

'And I'm not answering.' The glow imparted by the rum had faded completely now, leaving her strangely devoid of emotion. She had never felt as level-headed as she did at that moment. 'The only thing I am going to say ... and that's just to set the record straight ... is that the last time I saw Ian was the night he told me he was married. You can believe it or not, just as you like, but it happens to be the truth. Now can we go? It's gone three-fifteen.'

He didn't move, just sat there looking at her across the width of the table with an indecipherable expression. 'I'd like to believe you,' he said at last. 'Only if I do that makes my brother-in-law a liar twice over.'

'He didn't lie to me. He just didn't tell me he had a wife.' She wanted to convince him, yet could not help feeling that in doing so she was letting Ian down badly. 'Did your sister guess he was seeing someone, or did he tell her himself?'

'I'm not sure. So far I've only had one rather garbled letter from her which didn't really give any details. If she didn't guess, he'd have done better to keep the whole affair to himself.'

'Isn't that rather like saying a man should be able to do as he wants so long as his wife doesn't find out?'

'No, it isn't. All I'm saying is he might have saved the two of them a whole lot of trouble by keeping his mouth shut.' He looked at her for a long moment.

'Maybe he thought you might see fit to inform her after he'd given you the brush-off.'

She swallowed on the hard little lump in her throat. 'Thanks, I had enough on my plate.'

Something flickered in his eyes. 'Were you in love with Ian?'

'Not quite. I was ... working up to it, perhaps. We had a lot in common.' She assessed his expression with a wry little smile. 'You're still not sure about me, are you?'

'It's a case of getting used to a whole new set of ideas. I simply took it for granted that he'd had encouragement from you. They've only been married a bit more than a year. It normally takes rather longer than that for a man to start thinking about adding a few side dishes to the main course.' The last with cynicism.

She said thoughtfully, 'I suppose in a way he did get encouragement from me. He seemed so ...'

'So what?' he prompted, and she knew from the way he said it that he wasn't going to let her leave it in the air like that.

'So much in need of someone to talk to—or even just to be with,' she finished with slight defiance. 'It's maybe none of my business, but are you sure your sister's marriage was a happy one even before all this happened?'

'As sure as I can be, seeing the two of them only about three times a year.' His tone was short. 'June may still be a bit on the immature side, but she certainly never gave the impression that anything might be going wrong. In fact, when I was with them in September I'd have said she was as crazy about him as she ever was.' He frowned down into his glass. 'Did he discuss her with you at all?'

'No, he didn't. He just told me he was married, that he was sorry, and then went. That was just over three weeks ago.'

A certain light of understanding crept into his gaze. 'Was that why you came out here?'

'Yes. And ran slap bang into you.'

'That must have been quite a shock.'

'It was ... especially when I realised what kind of a person you'd taken it for granted I must be.'

'You can hardly blame me for that, considering your reactions.'

'Which way would you have expected me to react?' Alex demanded. 'Would you have been prepared to listen if I'd attempted to explain my side of it there and then?'

'Probably not,' he admitted after a moment. 'I was pretty intent on taking advantage of a heaven-sent opportunity to put you through it.'

She hardly dared say it. 'And now?'

He made a noncommittal movement. 'Rome wasn't built in a day. You've implanted enough of a doubt to give me pause for reflection, but ...' he eyed her a brief thoughtful moment ... 'I suppose what I need for a clincher is confirmation from Ian himself. I don't see why he shouldn't make some small amends by giving it either.'

If it hadn't been for that business with the pendant Alex was almost certain he would have given her the benefit of the doubt there and then. As it was, he had to believe her either a liar or incredibly naïve, and she had to admit that outward appearances belied the latter assessment. Instinct told her to leave it at that until Ian had confirmed her story—providing he was willing to do so. She had an odd premonition that it might not turn out to be quite so simple.

'Does he know I'm here on the *Andromeda*?' she asked.

'I imagine June will have passed on the news by now. I wrote and told her about it the day I heard myself, which was only a couple of days before you arrived.' His tone changed a little. 'I've been expecting a letter from her all week.'

'Perhaps she's decided to sort out her own problems and leave you to deal with this end of it. You'll be able to tell her that her faith in you didn't go unrewarded.'

A small reluctant smile touched his lips. 'I'm not going to apologise for being rough on you. You brought that on yourself. Even in different circumstances there'd still have been antagonism between us. And you know why.'

'Do I?' Green eyes were suddenly veiled.

'Sure. Because you basically resent any man you can't put down. That could be why you cottoned on to Ian. He was never a particularly strong character.'

Alex gave him a long straight look. 'You don't really like him very much, do you?'

'Liking has nothing to do with it. He just isn't the kind of man June should have married.'

'Then I'm surprised you allowed it.'

'She was of age; I couldn't have stopped it.' Eyes glinting, he added, 'And playing the heavy brother never came easily, surprisingly enough. Bringing up a girl of twelve was a responsibility I could well have done without.'

'How old is she now?'

'Twenty-one.'

Which would have made him about the mid-twenties when he took over that responsibility, Alex reflected. Hardly an ideal age to be landed with such a task. She wanted to ask if he'd kept June with him during those years, but decided against it. Together with Sally Freeman, that made three of them who had all undergone the same deprivation of a normal family life. That knowledge gave her a certain sense of affinity with Clay's young sister which even the present situation could not entirely cancel out.

'It can't have been easy for either of you,' she said.

He gave her a swift glance and seemed about to say something else, then apparently changed his mind, pushing back his chair instead with an abrupt movement. 'We'd better go and find that driver of yours before he comes looking for us.'

Pedro was drawing in along the side street where they had agreed to meet as they got there, his barely concealed yawn leading Alex to the conclusion that he had perhaps forgone his own lunch in favour of a rather more relaxed couple of hours.

They headed out of the city via the flyover which climbed rapidly towards the great pass through the mountains, settling down to a steady fifty miles an hour for the run down to La Guaira. The road was spectacular, at times cutting through long, brightly lit tunnels which reminded Alex of the one running under the Mersey back home, to emerge on the far side in yet another steep green valley topped by frowning crags.

With Pedro in the driving seat any conversation between the two of them in the back was limited to casual observations, but at no time could Alex lose her awareness of the man at her side. There was one tension-fraught moment when a particularly tight curve in the roadway sent her sliding across the seat without being able to do anything to stop her momentum. She felt Clay's hands on her waist steadying her as they had done in the cablecar earlier, but he made no attempt to put her back on her own side of the seat, holding her there lightly against him with his mouth only inches away from hers and a look in his eyes that made her pulses race. Being wanted physically was no new experience; Alex had long since learned to take such moments of recognition in her stride. Only this was different. This wasn't just *any* man. The depths of longing his touch alone could arouse in her were new and world-shaking.

'Sorry,' she said on as light a note as she could manage. 'I wasn't expecting that bend.' She was pressing herself away from him as she spoke, relieved when he let her go without protest yet desperately wanting him to keep her there at the same time. 'It might be better with the arm down.'

'Safer, anyway.' Whether the satire was directed at her or at himself it was impossible to guess. 'We'll be back on board inside ten minutes.'

It was just on five when they reached the docks. Alex was uncertain how to handle the question of payment, but Clay took the matter out of her hands. She had no way of knowing how large a tip he had included, but apparently it hadn't been a small one, for the Venezuelan was smiling as he tucked the notes away and made his farewells.

'You must let me know how much I owe you,' she offered tentatively as they made their way aboard the ship, and saw his mouth take on the familiar cynical slant.

'That's all right. I can afford it.'

'That's hardly the point.'

'Isn't it?' They had paused just inside the foyer, momentarily separated from the general flow of returning passengers. His regard was enigmatic. 'Did you insist on paying your way with Freeman too?'

'Well, no, of course not.' She floundered a little. 'That was ... different.'

'How?'

'Because he ... they ...' She stopped, made a small helpless gesture. 'I was their invited guest.'

'Then consider yourself *my* invited guest, if it makes it any easier. Either way I don't want to hear any more about paying.'

'All right.' There was no point in taking the matter any further. 'Thanks, anyway. It's been a day to remember.'

'Running away?' he said softly as she made a move to leave him there, and she forced herself to turn and look him in the eye.

'From what?'

'We both know what. The question is, what are we going to do about it?'

With a steadiness she was a long way from feeling, Alex said clearly, 'I don't know what *you're* going to do about anything, but I'm going below. Thanks again for the trip.'

One of the lift doors opened as she reached them, its only occupant peering out shortsightedly at the deck name plate fastened to the opposite bulkhead. 'Is this Carillon Deck?' she asked.

'No, it's Caribbean,' Alex told her. 'You've come down too far. I'm going up to Carillon myself.'

She stepped into the lift and pressed the button, refusing to allow herself even a glance towards the spot where she had left Clay standing as the doors slid closed again. If she could have hated him it might have helped. But she couldn't—at least not enough. To a man of his type there was only one kind of relationship a man had with a woman such as he still obviously believed she might be. The attraction existed, so why not indulge it? The fact that he could contemplate any kind of involvement at all with her, knowing what he did know, did not surprise her. Men seemed capable of totally separating their physical responses from their emotional ones. She only wished she possessed the same ability. It must make life a whole lot easier.

The cabin steward was coming along the alleyway as she turned in. He greeted her cheerfully, pausing to ease the tray he was carrying.

'You've got a visitor,' he informed her. 'Said she was a good friend of yours, so I let her wait in your cabin till you got back.' He grimaced as the telephone rang in the little cubbyhole a few yards away. 'Here we go again!'

He was gone before Alex could ask further questions. Perplexed, she carried on to her cabin and opened the door, pausing on the threshold as a pretty dark-haired girl rose slowly to her feet from the chair to stand there gazing at her with a curious mixture of hate and anticipation on her face.

'I don't suppose you ever expected to see me out here,' she said bitingly. 'I'm June Marriot. Your *lover's* wife!'

CHAPTER FIVE

IT was a moment or two before Alex could gather her wits sufficiently to speak.

'How did you get here?' she said at last, and thought even as she said it how irrelevant were the questions one asked at times like this. She shook her head. 'I mean ... why?'

'I'd have thought that would be obvious.' The younger girl spoke on a jerky note. 'It seemed about time I saw you for myself ... and told you what I thought of you! Women who go around stealing other women's husbands ought to be locked up, except that even that isn't bad enough for them!' Her hands clenched into fierce little fists at her sides as her voice lost its shaky control altogether. 'Aren't there enough men for you to ... to *entice* without going after someone like Ian?'

Alex let the door swing to behind her before answering, trying to think of something to say which would not inflame the situation any more than it already was. 'You seem to have got hold of the wrong idea about your husband and me,' she managed. 'Didn't Ian tell you?'

'Ian didn't need to tell me. I already knew.' June paused, drew in a quivering breath. 'A friend of mine saw you together in a restaurant and thought I should know about it. When I faced Ian with it he admitted the whole thing, so don't try to get out of it now!'

Alex said carefully, 'Exactly what did he tell you?'

'The truth. How you met in the park one lunchtime and you asked him to come and see you in a show.

How you kept on chasing him until he did and then wouldn't leave him alone. He admitted he was attracted to you, but he'd never have let it go as far as it did without encouragement, I'm quite sure of that! He'd never even looked at anyone else since we were married before you got your hooks into him!'

So Ian had lied to save what he could of his own skin. Alex wondered why she should have taken it for granted that he would have done otherwise. If she tried to tell this girl the real truth of the matter she doubted if she would be believed. And if she was, what then? The Marriots' marriage already appeared to be on the verge of foundering, considering June's presence here on the *Andromeda*. With Ian exposed twice over what chance of survival would it stand? Fatalistically she knew what she was going to have to do—the only thing she *could* do without having this mess on her conscience for the rest of her life. And she was going to need to be convincing.

Her shrug was as indifferent as she could make it. 'All right, so I tried to take him off you. As I obviously failed I can't see what all the fuss is about. You should be glad to have a husband who cares about you the way he does. I may have attracted him, but you're the one he wants. Be grateful for having it proved to you.'

The sudden swing of the door at her back almost caught her on the shoulder. When she turned Clay stood in the opening, face a taut mask. He let his gaze rest on her for just one brief moment before looking across at his sister, but it was enough to send her heart plummeting. There was no doubt that he had heard every word she had just uttered, and there was absolutely nothing she could do to refute them now. Not that it made any difference in the long run. June

would have passed on the admittance to him anyway
—one consideration she had not allowed herself time
to think about.

'What the devil are you doing here, June?' he
clipped. 'How did you get here anyway?'

'I flew in this morning. The shipping office made
all the arrangements.' She spoke quickly with a hint of
defiance. 'I knew you wouldn't have let me come if
I'd waited to ask you, so I made out that I wanted to
surprise you.' She paused before adding on a suddenly
tremulous note, 'I've left Ian.'

Clay came in and closed the door, properly this time,
his eyes narrowed to her face. 'Why wait three weeks to
decide?'

'I just couldn't stand it any more. Being in the same
house—even looking at him, when all the time I
kept seeing him with ... *her*!' The last with a hate-
filled glance in Alex's direction. 'Why should I be expected to make all the allowances?'

'It's not just a case of making allowances, it's keeping a sense of proportion. Does he know where you
are?'

'No, he doesn't.' She tossed the dark hair back out of
eyes gone stormy and mutinous. 'I just left him a note
saying I was going away and that I wouldn't be going
back.'

'That's something we'll talk about. The first thing
we'll do is get off a cable.'

'I should have known you'd be on his side.' Tears
weren't very far behind the resentful sparkle. 'You
think I'm just being silly taking it all so ... so seriously, don't you!'

'Stop it, June.' Clay spoke gently but with enough
authority to make his words carry weight. 'Of course

I'm not on Ian's side. What he's done he deserves to answer for ...' his glance towards Alex was a threat in itself ... 'along with others. But we can't leave him in the dark wondering what's happened to you, regardless. Do you have a cabin yet?'

'Yes, on the same deck as yours.'

'Then we'll go there ... after we've sent that cable.'

Alex moved to allow the younger girl room to pass. Between the three of them they seemed to fill the whole place. She felt quite numb for the moment, caught in a trap of her own making. There was nothing she could say, nothing she could do to make things any better. All she could hope for was that it would finish right here.

It was a forlorn hope; she had known in her heart that it would be. With his hand on his sister's arm, Clay looked back as they were leaving the cabin to say hardily, 'I'm not through with you by a long chalk, so don't imagine it. We'll do *our* sorting out later on.'

From somewhere Alex found the control to answer. 'I don't see much point in discussing the subject any further.'

The curl of his lip was deliberate. 'Neither do I.'

Alone again, she sank nervously to a seat in the chair June had so recently vacated. It had all come on her so quickly there had been no time to think things through. Yet she couldn't see what else she could have said or done, considering. The only person who could straighten things out with any conviction was Ian, and he was hardly likely to do that now.

Recalling Clay's parting shot she felt an involuntary little shiver run through her. Confined as she was to the ship for the coming thirty-six hours she had no way of avoiding that threatened confrontation, and she needed no warning that it would not be a pleasant affair. She would simply have to bluff it through regardless of what it cost her. And maybe after that Clay would be prepared to leave her alone at last. She tried to shut out the utter desolation that thought brought her.

The ship sailed promptly at six, moving out majestically to the open sea on the first leg of her four-hundred-and-fifty-mile journey to Barbados. At six-thirty Alex got up from the bed where she had been supposedly resting, and halfheartedly searched through her wardrobe for a dress to wear to dinner, although she had never felt less like eating. Unable to stay in the cabin just waiting for something to happen, she made her way up to Beach Deck as soon as she was ready. She hardly knew whether to be glad or sorry when Philip detached himself from a small group in the Pool Bar and came outside to where she had stopped by the rail.

'Had a good day?' he asked.

'Excellent, thanks.' She forced a light note. 'I'm looking forward to seeing more of the place next time round.'

There was a pause before he said, 'I hear you came back with Clay.'

'Yes, we bumped into each other on the mountain top and he offered to show me some of the best tourist spots.' Alex found time to wonder at her ability to sound so casual about it. 'I was very impressed by Caracas.'

'So was I the first time I saw it.' He grinned suddenly. 'You know, you've got Marian Lee practically foaming at the mouth! She was with Clay and one or two others from the ship when he ditched them in favour of you. I'd watch out for her or you might find yourself shoved overboard one dark night!'

If Marian Lee were all she had to worry about she would be laughing, Alex thought wryly as she made some appropriately light reply. She wondered if Clay really would give the dancer the brush-off as he had intimated. Not that it mattered one way or the other now.

'Come and have a drink with the boys,' invited Philip. 'Those off duty usually congregate up here about this time.'

'Then they won't want a woman intruding.'

'You must be joking. They told me to come out and fetch you in. You don't seem to realise your own popularity!'

Alex took a quick glance over her shoulder in the direction of the group clearly visible behind the glass frontage, saw the Scottish officer she had danced with that first night raised a cheery hand in acknowledgement and came to a decision without further consideration. Right now she needed something to take her out of herself, and Gerry Duncan would certainly do that.

'You talked me into it,' she said.

She was greeted with warming enthusiasm by all four officers, drawn into their midst as if she belonged there. Philip got her a Martini, standing close by her side as if to indicate his own rather closer claim as the one who had persuaded her to join them.

'I thought you were supposed to circulate among the passengers,' she remarked after a few minutes, sensing the glances their little group was receiving from the latter. She had to laugh at Gerry's comical grimace.

'Oh, come on, it can't be that bad!'

'Not after a few of these. That's why we leave the chat till later.' His glance moved beyond her and lit up afresh. 'Ladies' night tonight, is it? Who's the little lassie Clay's got in tow?'

Alex froze as brother and sister hove into view, her eyes fixed on the slender-stemmed glass in her hand. She heard Clay making introductions and forced herself to look up and acknowledge the two of them, meeting the cold grey eyes with creditable composure.

June was looking exceptionally pretty in blue and white, her dark hair brushed into a shining cap about her small face. She was smiling and looked without a care in the world at the moment. Only when her glance clashed briefly with Alex's did the sparkle fade a little, then her chin lifted in a gesture which conveyed far more than words. In spite of everything, Alex could only admire her spirit.

It was both a relief and a release when the time came that she could plausibly excuse herself to go down to dinner. Everyone else, it appeared, had eaten at the earlier sitting. Once away from the bar, however, she acknowledged her total lack of interest in food of any kind and decided instead on an early night, thankful for the freedom from professional demands which enabled her to do so. She felt tired and dispirited, aware of a deep-seated ache which was going to get worse before it got better. Everything had gone wrong and she could see no way of improving matters. Sleep seemed the only attractive proposition available.

After seeing Clay again in the bar she had somehow not anticipated any further contact before the morning. She had been lying awake for what seemed like hours when the knock came on the outer door, and even then she told herself it would only be the steward —although it was unlikely he would come to the cabin without being summoned.

Heart racing, she got out of the bed and pulled on a wrap before crossing the few feet of carpet, pausing with her hand on the knob and a churning sensation inside.

'Who is it?' she asked, and heard an impatient movement on the far side of the door.

'Who else are you expecting?'

She swallowed thickly. 'I'm already in bed. Whatever you've got to say it can wait till morning.'

The pause lasted no more than a second or two. 'I don't give a damn where you are. Either you open the door or I'll fetch the spare key and let myself in.'

Alex looked at the flimsy little catch which was supposed to make the cabin secure against unauthorised entry while occupied, then slowly drew it back. Clay had a hand resting on the jamb, the other thrust into his trouser pocket. He was still in uniform, the white jacket emphasising the dark tan of his skin.

'An official visit?' she asked with what coolness she could muster, and saw his jaw visibly tauten.

'I can take it off if it bothers you.' He stepped over the threshold, forcing her to move back away from the door, then closing it behind him and leaning his weight against it as he surveyed her. 'Did you think I didn't mean what I said earlier?'

'Not at all.' Now that the moment was upon her Alex found herself suddenly ready to meet it, keyed up but no longer apprehensive. Let him say what he liked, he wasn't going to see her cringe. Neither was she going to waste any time trying to explain her motives, because that was what it would be—a complete waste.

'I imagine you're more than accustomed to taking up cudgels on your sister's behalf.'

'Someone has to.'

'Why? She's of age, as you pointed out yourself only this afternoon. Why not try treating her like an adult for once?'

His eyes were dangerous. 'Attack the best means of defence—is that it? I shouldn't take it too far, if I were you. You've already proved yourself a liar, don't be a fool into the bargain.'

'There's an old saying—trite but true—about being hanged for a sheep as well as for a lamb.' She had her back to the wardrobe fitting, one closed fist pressed against the side of her waist, almost as though clutching a pain. 'You made up your mind about me before we even met, so why should I care what you might think of me now? Before you start laying the blame at anyone's door look to your own contribution. Maybe if you hadn't been quite so ready to take over her troubles in the past she'd have been better equipped to meet this one. I'd be willing to bet she never made one real decision in her life without your invaluable aid!'

'A good try,' he said. 'But not good enough. You're not going to wriggle out of this that way. You might even be right up to a point, only that doesn't happen to be the issue at stake. What we have to settle is a matter between the two of us alone.'

She was silent, watching him warily, alive to the silky menace of that latter statement. They were like two prize-fighters, she thought: circling; feinting, watching for an opening. Only she was fighting out of her weight, and they both knew it. No matter what she said or did it was going to make little difference to the outcome he had already decided upon. The question was, what he actually did intend.

'I'd say it was already settled,' she finally got out. 'You've proved your instincts about me right, and told me what I am. Isn't that enough?'

'No, it isn't enough.' The line of his mouth was inflexible. 'Remember what I once said about putting you where you belong?'

She tensed, her fingers curling into her palms. 'I remember.'

'Right.' He came away from the door with a deliberation more nerve-tingling than any sudden movement. 'So that's where we'll sort out our differences, in a way we'll both understand.'

She stood her ground as he came towards her, eyes dark in the taut whiteness of her face. 'I'll see you in hell first!'

His smile was slow. 'You might, at that!'

Alex struck out at him as he reached for her, only to have her wrists seized and pinned behind her back in a grip she couldn't break. His mouth was hard and demanding, crushing all protest and bringing the blood pounding into her ears. She felt the edge of the bed against the back of her knees, and then he was pressing her down into the pillows, looming over her like some avenging devil as he blocked her attempts to twist free of him. He wanted her to fight him, she realised. He wanted to see fear in her eyes, to have the excuse to subdue her forcibly. Well, that was one satisfaction she could deny him, no matter what it cost her.

She forced herself to stop the futile struggling, to go limp in his grasp as though unable to fight any more. Mockery curving his lips, he found her mouth again, claiming possession in a way that set every fibre of her being alight. Clay knew too much about women; too much about everything. It took every ounce of will-power she had to remain unresponsive, but she managed it, lying there motionless until he finally lifted his head to look at her.

Her breathing was shaky, but she kept her gaze steady and unflinching as she looked back at him. 'Have you proved what you set out to prove,' she asked, 'or was that just the preliminary bout?'

A spark of unwilling admiration crept into his eyes. 'You just don't know how to give in, do you?'

'Not if giving in means accepting anything you care to dish out. You came down here tonight to make a point. Well, all right, so you made it. Where brute strength is concerned you have the edge any day. I promise to remember it.'

It was impossible to stop the small gasp of pain as his hands tightened cruelly. 'Just keep on like that and you're going to find out what brute strength really is! You're not lying there like the original ice-maiden because that's the way you feel. I could time your pulse rate from here!'

Alex bit back the retort trembling on her lips, said instead, 'So what?'

His eyes gleamed. 'So ... this.'

The touch of his lips, soft and sensuous against the skin of her throat, brooked no denial this time. She closed her eyes, feeling the involuntary response of her body and knowing that he felt it too. His hands had lost their hardness but were even more so instruments of torture, drawing her on to forget all but the exquisite sensation of the moment, the pleasure that was almost pain. She had to draw on all her reserves to find the strength of mind to say no to the need rising so desperately in her before it was too late. This was Clay Anderson making love to her: a man she hated and who hated her. Whatever power he might have to stir her she had to remember that!

'That's enough,' she said huskily. 'Clay, please ...'

It was a moment before he spoke, and when he did it was apparent how close she had come to being ignored. 'Capitulation?' he asked on a hard note of mockery.

'If you want to call it that.' She had little choice and the danger was still present, but she refused to appear completely beaten. 'No one's denying your expertise.'

He looked at her for a long threatening moment. 'I wonder just what it *would* take to break you,' he said at last. 'Maybe we should carry on and find out.'

Her heart was thudding against her rib cage. Was that what she wanted? she wondered fleetingly: to have the decision taken out of her hands? If so she was certainly going the right way about it.

'I don't want to carry on,' she said, 'and I don't think you ever meant to.'

It was hard to define his thoughts from his expression. 'I didn't?'

'No, you didn't. You'd hardly be likely to risk your job that far.'

'Why assume there'd be any risk?'

'They couldn't ignore a complaint of that nature, and you know it.'

'Your word against mine?' His tone was dry. 'After Monday it's been generally assumed there's something going between us anyway. A woman doesn't spend a whole day with a man she can't stand near her. Not that you'd have put in any complaint. You'd rather put your head in a noose than admit to having a man get the better of you!'

Her throat hurt. 'You don't know me as well as you seem to think you do. In your case I'd have considered it well worth it.'

'Maybe.' He let go of her and sat up. 'We'll never know, will we?'

'I know.' She said it with more conviction than she felt. 'You're going anyway.'

He paused in the act of rising from the bed. 'You want me to stay?'

'No!' Alex caught her lip between her teeth. 'You know that's not what I meant.'

'Then *say* what you mean.' He ran his eyes over her, taking his time about it. 'I wouldn't need much persuading.' The broad shoulders lifted ironically at the expression which swiftly crossed her face. 'It's a matter of priorities. Right now I'm in no particular mood to start sorting mine out, so watch the smart remarks.'

Alex had none left. Reaction was setting in, making it difficult to control the trembling in her limbs. She came up on one elbow when he got to his feet, fighting to preserve what command of the situation she still possessed. 'Assuming I've learned my lesson, do we take the matter as finished now?'

He took a moment to reply, studying her with cynicism. 'The day you get off this ship for good it will finish,' he said. 'Sleep tight. You'll need all your stamina for tomorrow's performance.'

Alone again at last, Alex leaned her head weakly against the bulkhead and considered the implications of that parting shot. Ten more weeks of Clay's relentless enmity would be more than she could take; she had already had more than she could take. This was what she got for running away in the first place. She should have stayed where she belonged and relegated her relationship with Ian to its proper place. Instead she was right here in the thick of a situation she could see no way out of, except by running away again. And how would she explain *that* to Barney? His reaction could only be predictable: if Ian's brother-in-law was making life aboard the *Andromeda* intolerable for her then the matter should be referred to a higher authority. Little more than a week ago her own solution might very well have been the same, only between then and now stretched a whole chapter of events which made any appeal to a third party almost impossible. All she had had to do tonight, for instance, was to call for help. But she hadn't. And why?

The answer to that was something she didn't want to think about.

Despite his threats to the contrary, Clay made no further attempt to approach her in any personal sense during the following few days, and having learned something of his duty routine during the previous week Alex was able to steer clear of any direct contact herself. When she wasn't with her brother, June seemed always to be in company with one or other of his fellow officers. Like a protection squad, Alex thought ruefully, except that June wasn't the one who needed it.

Over the course of the week she found herself spending more and more time with Philip, aware that by doing so she might be offering the very encouragement she had hoped to avoid, but unable to bring herself to turn aside the only real friend she felt she had on board ship.

'There's a rumour going around that you were involved with Clay's sister's husband in some way,' he said to her once when they were together on the upper sun deck. 'I ... well, I thought you ought to know.'

Marian Lee, Alex surmised. It could be no one else. Clay certainly would not be likely to have circulated that particular item of news. What the dancer hoped to gain she couldn't begin to imagine. Whatever her motives, the other must have forfeited any chance she had ever had of getting closer to Clay. As Alex knew to her cost, he neither forgot nor forgave very easily.

'Are you asking me if it's true?' she returned bluntly, and saw Philip's face colour a little.

'If it is I'm sure you wouldn't have meant it to happen that way. You're not that kind of person.'

She put out a hand and impulsively covered his. 'You are nice, Phil. Thanks. I only wish others had your faith!'

He turned his hand over so that hers was underneath, holding it there on the edge of the lounger in a way that made it difficult to withdraw it. 'Is Clay riding you about it? Is that why he followed you on Monday?'

'He didn't follow me. He got separated from his own party by accident.' In retrospect Alex didn't believe it either, but she had no intention of involving Philip in any part of this. She smiled at him, and gently extracted her hand. 'It will all blow over. These things always do.'

'I can't see how with his sister right here on board. I'm surprised he agreed to her coming out here as things were.' He paused. 'It really was a terrific coincidence, wasn't it ... I mean, you coming all this way and then running into Clay. Obviously you couldn't have known about him or you wouldn't have been so puzzled that first day when he was acting so oddly with you.'

'No, I didn't, and yes, it was a coincidence. They happen more often in real life than they do in fiction, if anything.' She wished he would leave the subject alone; she wished everyone would leave it alone! She sat up, adjusting her sunglasses. 'I think I've had about enough for this afternoon. I don't want to look like a broiled chicken tonight.'

'You've already got too good a tan for that,' he commented. 'You won't go red now. I always thought blondes couldn't take the sun at all.'

She said lightly, 'Maybe I've got a thick skin.'

'Well, whatever, it looks great under the spotlight. Will you be wearing that floaty thing?'

She grinned. 'That floaty thing, as you call it, happens to be just about the most expensive item in my whole wardrobe, so refer to it with respect! I wasn't planning to wear it tonight, but I suppose there's no reason why I shouldn't.'

'Great. Jimmy Keen's saying you'll wow them with that new number.'

'I hope he's right.' Alex tried to put enthusiasm into her voice. She had never felt as indifferent about a performance as she did now thinking about tonight's, and she had no right to be feeling that way. The true professional never allowed personal problems to get in the way, no matter how pressing. If she wanted to get across to that audience tonight she was going to have to put Clay Anderson right out of her mind—and that was easier said than done.

Remembering that last week she had been called upon to share a cabin with Marian Lee on cabaret night, she waited as long as she dared before going to change, and was thankful to find the cabin empty. The black dress Philip had spoken of hung ready on its hanger where she had put it earlier, the filmy overlayers softly draped about the silk sheath which formed the base. Only when her make-up was applied and she came to put it on did she see the jagged tear extending the whole length of the front.

Dismayed, she examined the damage, finally coming to the conclusion that it couldn't possibly have got there during the transfer from her own cabin. Which meant that it had either been there before she took it from the wardrobe, or had been inflicted right here in the dressing room. And if that latter, then only one person could have done it. Marian Lee!

With only a bare five minutes to go before she was due on there was no time for dwelling on the matter. Neither was there going to be time to fetch another dress from her cabin. Alex hesitated only a second or two before reaching for a pair of scissors and starting work on the top layers of the dress, ruthlessly stripping them away and hoping that any left-over threads wouldn't show. Finished, she got into what was left of the garment, sliding up the zip and viewing herself in the mirror with not a little doubt. On the face of it the dress was modest enough in design with its high, diamanté-faced neckline and long tight sleeves, but it was the way it fitted which caused her concern. Within its original cocoon of gossamer net it had formed an occasionally glimpsed silhouette against the beam of a spotlight—what Barney always referred to as eyebait. Shorn of that protecting shroud it left little to the imagination, following every curve of her body with loving care, the material so fine it gave an illusion of semi-transparency. She felt practically naked right here in the privacy of the dressing room. What she would feel like out there under the concerted gaze of more than two hundred pairs of eyes she daren't imagine, but she had no choice. It was either this or not going on at all, and she was not about to give Marian the satisfaction of that latter course.

Clay was talking with Kreenia, the Yugoslav magician who had just finished his own act, when she rounded the corner to bring her backstage. He saw her at the same moment that she saw him, and stopped in mid-sentence to look her over from head to toe with an expression which made her writhe.

'Aiming to impress the masses?' he queried.

The Yugoslav was looking at her too, though with a rather different expression. 'The masses are fortunate,' he said in his thickly accented English on a decidedly appreciative note. 'No woman should hide such a beautiful body!'

Alex tried vainly to control the wave of heat which ran up under her skin. She saw surprise followed by sudden amusement in Kreenia's eyes, and knew that he at least recognised her reticence if not quite understanding it.

'I'm on,' she said hastily as the orchestra struck up with her opening number. She didn't look at Clay again as she slipped past the two men to step out into the circle of light waiting to receive her.

Afterwards Alex was never certain whether it was her rendering of the latest British release or the dress which gained the most approval, but the applause left nothing to be desired. She took two encores before they would finally let her go, coming off both exhausted and exhilarated after twenty-five minutes of all-out effort to meet almost face to face with Marian waiting with the other dancers to go on for the final bows.

Seeing the glittering malice in the other girl's eyes, Alex knew her suspicions had been well founded. She said softly, 'You should have done a better job while you were about it,' and carried on past before the dancer could reply.

Heading for the dressing room after the finale, she was thankful to see no sign of Clay. The relief was shortlived, however. When she opened the door he was in there waiting for her, with the remnants of her earlier work with the scissors spread out across the chair.

'What happened?' he demanded without preamble.

She looked from the chair to his face stonily. 'Maybe I just wanted a change.'

'Come again. No woman deliberately rips up a dress like this one was to get something like *that*. I'm no expert, but I'd say the original must have cost you close on a hundred and fifty.'

'A hundred and eighty, to be exact.' She came further into the cabin, leaving the door open. 'So it got damaged and I had to think fast. It was either this or not going on at all.'

His eyes had narrowed. 'How did it get damaged?'

'I snagged the front edge and tore it trying to pull it free.' She shrugged with assumed nonchalance. 'One of those unfortunate things. I'll have to get another.' She paused before tagging on, 'On the other hand, I could always stick with what's left of it. It didn't do me much harm out there tonight.'

'You don't need any gimmicks.' His voice was tight. 'All that little number did for you tonight was cause a distraction. And while we're still on the subject, this tear of yours was started off with scissors. Can you explain that too?'

Alex held his gaze. 'I don't have to explain it.'

He drew in an impatient breath. 'If this happened the way I think it did I want to know about it. It wouldn't be the first time we've had professional jealousy on board.'

'In which case you'll realise that the best way of dealing with it is to ignore it.'

'Not on your life. This time it was only a dress, next time it might be more serious.'

'My, my,' she mocked. 'Drama on the High Seas! Why don't you try your hand at writing the scenario?'

His eyes glinted dangerously. 'If I try my hand at anything you'll be the first to know about it! I'm asking you for the last time. Did somebody rip up that dress for you?'

The time for bravado was certainly not now. Alex forced herself to answer steadily. 'I suppose somebody must have. What can you do about it?'

'I can guarantee it won't happen again.'

'How?'

'That's my affair.' He moved to the door. 'You'll have this place to yourself in future.'

'That's a relief.' She didn't turn her head. 'Would it be too much to ask why you were here in the first place?'

He paused in the doorway to look back at her, irony in the line of his mouth. 'You'll never be sure, will you?'

Marian still hadn't returned when Alex was ready to go. She took both parts of the damaged dress with her, pushing them out of sight in one of her suitcases until she could get rid of them. There had been a tentative arrangement that she join Philip in the Calypso Club after the show. But she no longer felt up to making merry into the small hours. She wondered how Clay would see fit to deal with the dancer, but could reach no conclusions on that score. Nothing about that man was predictable. That was the danger. It was also, a small inner voice suggested, a part of his fascination. And that, Alex acknowledged, was a danger of quite another kind.

CHAPTER SIX

It was seeing the fast-becoming-familiar San Juan waterfront again the following morning which reminded Alex of the pendant for the first time in days. She had done nothing about writing that letter, and the problem still existed. It was possible, she realised, that there would be a letter for her from Glenn when the mail was brought on board. A week had passed since his return home—time for him to have received her letter and written back. In a way that would make things even more difficult.

Philip joined her at the rail. 'Can't stop more than a minute. The Immigration people just came on board and I'm down to help out. You know what chaos it is down there.'

Alex did. She had gone through it herself. If any would-be illegal immigrants managed to slip through the net the American authorities here laid out they would be very lucky. It was woe betide anyone who didn't have their papers in perfect order.

'I waited for you last night,' he went on. 'You said you'd come up when you were ready.'

'I said I'd try. Sorry I couldn't make it after all. I was just too tired.'

'Oh, well, there's always...'

'Aren't you supposed to be down with Immigration?' The voice came from behind them on a note which jerked Philip upright away from the rail.

'I was just on my way.'

'I'm sure you were.' Clay lifted an interrogative eyebrow when his subordinate continued to stand there. 'Well?'

Alex waited until the younger man was out of earshot before saying caustically, 'I'll bet that made your morning. He only stopped to say hallo.'

'Fine. I simply hurried up his goodbyes.' He came to lean where Philip had been, looking down on the activity below. 'Looks like the overnight flight was early. Thinking of going ashore?'

She shook her head. 'I saw quite a bit of it last week ... the town itself, at least.'

'With the Freemans?'

Her chin came up. 'Yes.'

Her tone was meant to discourage, but it didn't. She hadn't really expected it to. 'Heard from him since?'

'No, I haven't.' She hoped he wouldn't ask about the pendant. Without really intending to she heard herself adding, 'How did the detective work go last night?'

'There was little needed.' The pause was brief but weighty. 'It seems I owe you an apology about that dress. All things considered, it was pretty quick thinking on your part.'

Her surprise held not a little suspicion. Clay apologising to her—there had to be a catch in it somewhere. 'Don't mention it,' she said. 'Short of holding up the whole show while I got myself something else to wear it was the only solution.' She paused, not looking at him. 'Although I suppose you could always have put Marian Lee on as a stopgap.'

The hands curving over the rail showed suddenly white about the knuckles. 'You don't pull any punches, do you?'

'You might say I've had a good teacher. What did you expect—gratitude?' The words said themselves, derived from a sudden desperate desire to keep the distance between them from narrowing in any way. There was safety of a kind in hostility: she could cope with that, anticipate at least some of his moves. He held too much sway over her emotions to risk any kind of relaxation in his company. She fixed her gaze on the file of incoming passengers passing across the gangway two decks below where she stood, focusing on the tall man at this moment being greeted by the officer at the far end without really seeing anything but the shape of his head outlined against the huge packing case immediately behind him. The shape of his head . . .

Beside her Clay made a sudden movement. 'So that's what you were waiting here for,' he said with soft comprehension. 'Like a puppet on a string. Congratulations!'

Alex gathered herself together, still unable to believe the evidence of her own eyes. That was Glenn down there. Glenn! But he'd only been gone a week. What on earth . . .

'I had no idea he was going to be here,' she denied. 'He . . . must have flown down on business.'

'If he has it's right here on board. That's a ticket he's handing in, not a visitor's pass.' His tone was heavy with satire. 'We'll have to arrange some special entertainment for him. How about "hunt the emerald"?'

Alex gripped the rail as he swung round and strode off. Everyone seemed to be conspiring to make a liar out of her. Why *had* Glenn come back? And what was she going to say to him now that he was here? She couldn't even begin to straighten out her confusion.

As if by instinct he lifted his head as he stepped on to the gangway and saw her standing at the rail. His smile and the quick wave of his hand in greeting left very little room for doubt regarding his reasons for returning to San Juan. Alex waved back, and heard him call out for her to stay where she was. Then he vanished into the body of the ship.

It could only have been minutes, yet it seemed like an hour before she saw him emerge on to the open deck some small distance aft. Somehow she made her feet carry her forward to greet him, found her mouth widening into a smile and her hands going out in response to his.

'Glenn, I can't believe it! I imagined a possible letter, but hardly a personal visit!'

'Not just a visit,' he said. 'I'm sailing with you.' He let go of her hand to take her by the shoulders and draw her towards him, bending his head and kissing her as naturally as if they had known one another for years. 'I had to come back. I haven't been able to concentrate on anything this last week.' He was smiling as he said it, searching her features with an expression she found both dismaying and heartwarming at the same time. 'Your letter clinched the decision for me.

Reading it I knew I had to see you again ... and soon. We have a lot to talk about, Alex.'

'We have?' She was trying hard to remember just what she had put in that letter. It had been written straight off the top, admittedly, but she was certain that nothing she had said could have elicited such a response. Yet he was here. What they did have to talk about was the pendant, she acknowledged. There was no getting round that difficult topic. She had to explain her mistake before they went any further.

'I've taken a suite this trip,' Glen was saying now. 'Can we go there and do our talking? The decks are liable to get rather public.'

Alex was in agreement there. She could cope with this whole matter better in private. 'Which deck?'

He smiled. 'This one. As a matter of fact, I believe we're standing practically outside it, but we'll have to go back through the ship to reach it.'

The Cumberland Suite was magnificent, occupying the starboard quarter of the cabin space with a superb view for'ard through the two large square ports. The sitting room was carpeted in deep amber, with cream wool upholstery on the couches and chairs against bulkheads panelled in teak. The cost, even for a week, was extortionate, Alex knew. This was real luxury living with every convenience to hand.

She stood there in the middle of the expanse of thick-piled carpet as Glenn closed the outer door, wondering how to broach the subject of the pendant in the least hurtful way. Glenn took the initiative out of her hands, coming purposefully across to her.

'Now,' he said, 'I can kiss you properly. The way I wanted to so badly the day we left.'

Alex was too uncertain of herself to consider protesting, and after a moment she no longer wished to do so. There was something infinitely comforting in the feel of Glenn's arms about her, in the warm possessiveness of his lips. With a man like this a woman could feel needed as well as wanted; protected and secure. Without thinking about it she slipped her own arms around his neck and responded in kind, closing her mind to all comparisons and letting the present take its course. When they finally broke apart she felt bereft, exposed once more to outside influences.

'That was even more than I'd hoped for,' he said. He made no attempt to conceal the unsteadiness in his voice. 'Alex, you're the most wonderful thing that's happened to me in years. Do you think you . . .'

'Please.' Her voice was unsteady too, though perhaps for different reasons. 'Glenn, can we just leave it as it is for now? I—I can't even think straight.'

'I'm taking things too fast,' he said wryly. 'I meant to let matters take a natural course. It isn't as if we're going to be short of time. I'm aiming to stay aboard the *Andromeda* until . . .' he stopped and gave a little smiling shrug . . . 'well, let's just say as long as necessary.'

'But you've seen it all before.' She was half laughing, half protesting. 'We cover exactly the same route week in, week out. They'll think you're mad!'

'Let them think what they like. I'm only interested in what you think.'

She was silent for a moment. 'And Sally?'

His expression underwent a subtle change. 'Sally knows how I feel.'

'That wasn't what I asked.'

'I know it wasn't.' He sounded faintly defensive. 'She doesn't believe I stand a chance with you. I suppose she thinks I'm too old for you, for one thing.'

At the present Alex did not feel like cogitating the pros and cons of that particular point. 'She's only seventeen. At that age even twenty-four is getting on a bit.' She moved away from him. 'What you're really saying is she doesn't like the idea of you chasing back down here to see someone you've only known a week. That's understandable, isn't it? After all, she's your daughter and you've apparently never been able to spare her much time.'

He winced, then smiled ruefully. 'I'm not going to try defending myself. I haven't been the best of fathers, and I know it. But you know, parental duty doesn't always come all that naturally to everybody, especially when there's no one to share it with. After Cassie died I wrapped myself in my work to try to keep from thinking about her. It didn't occur to me that Sally might be missing her too.' It was his turn to pause. 'I guess that's no recommendation in your eyes.'

Head bent, she said, 'We all make mistakes. I suppose the main thing is to recognise them.' She looked up then to meet his eyes fairly and squarely. 'Glenn, you're probably going to think me either a naïve fool or a liar, but I didn't realise that was a real emerald in the pendant when I wrote to thank you for it. It's been in the ship's safe since I discovered its value. Would you be very hurt if I asked you to take it back for the present?'

'Yes, I most certainly would.' He was obviously both surprised and perturbed by the request. 'The pendant was a small way of saying thank you for all you'd done to help bring Sally and me together, and I wouldn't dream of offering imitation stones to any woman. No matter what, I want you to keep it and wear it. Surely that isn't so much to ask?'

'You don't understand.' She tried again. 'If it hadn't

been real I could have worn it with pleasure. I did until someone...' Her voice tailed off.

'Until someone saw fit to put a cash value on it, I think you were going to say,' he finished for her. 'I can't see what difference it makes. It isn't as if I couldn't afford to buy it in the first place.'

'That isn't the point. It's...' She stopped again, made a helpless gesture. 'I can't explain.'

His gaze was suddenly shrewd. 'Did this certain someone happen to suggest anything else, by any chance? If so I'd like to have a few words with whoever it was and do some straightening out!'

She said quickly, 'No, it wasn't like that. Look, can we talk about it some other time? You ought to be getting along to see the maître d'hôtel before all the best tables go.'

He studied her a moment before accepting the too swift change of topic. 'I'll do that if you'll agree to share a table with me while I'm on board. Tonight, though, I thought we might go ashore and sample the town's high spots before we sail.' His brows lifted humorously. 'To put it in the accepted vernacular, how does that grab you?'

Alex made an appropriate answer, aware that the question of the pendant had only been shelved but willing to let it ride for now. It would be a change to get away from the ship for a while. And it would keep her out of Clay's way.

Keeping out of Clay's way became a major occupation during the next week. At Alex's suggestion they spent most of the daylight hours ashore in the various ports, discovering places they'd missed the first time round. In Martinique they took the ferry across the bay and bathed from a beach almost too beautiful to be real. Out here, with only the breeze among the palm leaves and the gentle whisper of the sea lapping silver-white sand to break the blue-hazed stillness it was not difficult to imagine oneself as a castaway on some far-flung desert island. As Glenn was moved to remark, being a beachcomber in this part of the world couldn't be bad.

He said much the same thing on St Thomas, lying comfortably in one of the loungers spread along the curving, palm-lined beach at Lime Tree Bay with a tall glass of iced rum punch to hand, imperturbed by Alex's dry retort.

'There are ways and ways,' he responded lazily. 'I suppose there's nothing to stop me from retiring right now and doing this for the rest of my life.' He opened his eyes but didn't turn his head. 'Or I could follow you around the world. I wouldn't expect you to give up your career if you married me, Alex. I'd do everything in my power to extend it.'

'Does that mean you won't if I don't?' she asked, try-ing to infuse a lighter note. 'That comes under the heading of bribery.'

'I don't mind what you call it if it gets you to say yes.'

She said softly, 'Glenn, we barely know one another. How can you possibly be so sure you want to marry me after less than a fortnight together?'

'I know. I knew after only a couple of days. It hap-pens like that sometimes.'

'Is that how it happened with your first wife?'

'Not quite as quickly but just as surely.' There was a slight hesitation before he went on, 'I hope you won't take this the wrong way, but in some ways you're rather like Cassie was at your age. Oh, not in looks, maybe. Its something in the way you hold your head when you laugh ... even the way you look at me sometimes.'

Her throat felt tight. 'You loved her very much, didn't you?'

'Yes, I did.' He reached out and took hold of her hand, sincerity in every line of his face. 'And I love you very much, Alex. You must believe that.'

She must have made a satisfactory reply because he relaxed again, but inside she knew no such conviction. What Glenn was really looking for was a replacement for the wife he had loved and lost, and she doubted herself capable of stepping into anyone else's shoes and making them fit. There was temptation in what he was offering her, only without enough feeling on her part it would never work out. She was extremely fond of Glenn and she respected him as a person, but she didn't love him—not yet anyway.

She transferred to the pool side just behind the beach while Glenn went to the hotel to arrange about lunch, amused by the antics of the semi-tamed iguanas living free among the surrounding trees. She was watching one particularly inquisitive youngster edging its way towards the nearest small group of humans when she became aware of having company. Clay was wearing brief white trunks and had a cotton shirt slung over one shoulder. Standing there looking down at her with the familiar sardonic smile on his face he epitomised male dominance in exactly the way he had done the night he had come to her cabin. Alex felt the same quivering response start up inside her and could do nothing to stop it.

'Is this coincidence too?' she demanded, sitting up with a jerk and reaching instinctively for her beach robe. 'I suppose you just *happened* to be coming here today!'

'I always come here when we're in St Thomas. Most of the tourists go to Morning Star or Pineapple Beach.' He dropped to a seat on the end of her lounger, taking cigarettes and a lighter from the buttoned pockets of the shirt he had been carrying and slinging the latter casually across the webbing. 'How's it going?'

'How is what going?'

'The romance with Freeman ... what else? You've been living in one another's pockets all week.'

She said stiffly, 'Isn't that our affair?' and wished she had found some other way of expressing herself as she saw his lip curl afresh.

'You know best. I don't suppose you've seen fit to fill him in on your past in any depth ... or is he willing to discount former associations?'

Alex felt suddenly sick. There was to be no letting up so far as Clay was concerned, that was apparent. He was determined to make her pay and keep on paying for what he believed she had done to his sister's marriage. Even if it had been true there was surely a limit to revenge?

'I take it that if I haven't you'll be more than willing to do it for me,' she said.

'Why bother? You can be pretty convincing when you set your mind to it.' The eyes watching the curl of smoke from the end of his cigarette were hard. 'On the other hand, I don't think you deserve too easy a ride with Freeman.'

'What does that mean?'

He shrugged. 'It depends to a great extent on what I find when I get back to the ship.' His glance met hers with calculation. 'I had a cable from Ian this morning. He's flying in this afternoon. I've left June back there to meet him. Letting her sort out her own problems, I think you called it.'

Alex kept her face carefully expressionless. 'I hope it works out.'

'So do I.' There was a threat in the way he said it. 'Providing you keep away from them there's a chance.'

'If you feel that way about it I'd have thought they would have been better off getting together somewhere else.'

'I agree. Unfortunately, Ian doesn't appear to have considered that particular aspect, which brings me to the conclusion that you may be the bigger draw. It will be interesting to find out.' His glance strayed beyond her. 'Your boy-friend's taking his time. Maybe he's found other interests up there.'

'If you saw where he went you must have been around before he left,' she responded with somewhat obvious logic, ignoring the last. 'Why didn't you come across while he was still here? I'm sure he'd have been delighted to see you.'

'Because I wanted to get you on your own,' with a warning glint. 'All right, so you've got him in the palm of your hand, I'll give you that. So far as he's concerned at present you're everything he wants in a woman. Is he everything you need in a man?'

The subtle emphasis was not lost on her. Pulse jerking, she said, 'Everything.'

'Then he's already made love to you?'

Despite herself she flushed. 'No, he damn well hasn't! Not the way you mean.'

'Then how do you know?' He was mocking. 'Money isn't everything, honey.'

'Neither is what you're talking about.'

'Sex is what I'm talking about. Why do women find

that word so hard to use? And don't try making out that it isn't important to you, because I know better. You might hate my guts, but I'd be willing to lay a bet that I could get more of a response from you right now than Freeman ever has.'

And he would win; she knew that as well as he did. But knowing it was one thing, admitting it another. With no fewer than a dozen other people around she felt safe enough to mock right back. 'Take your place amongst the world's great lovers, Mr Anderson. No doubt half of them were self-styled too!'

His laugh jarred. 'Don't wave any more red rags. This is a respectable hotel. If you want to gamble wait till we're back on the ship.' He got to his feet, scooping up his shirt in the same easy movement. 'If it's of any interest, Freeman is heading this way right now in something of a hurry. The possessive kind, is he?'

'Why don't you stay and ask him yourself?'

'Ease his doubts, you mean?' There was a cruel inflection. 'Tell him I've an urgent appointment, sorry to have missed him.'

Alex made herself relax back against the webbing as he moved away, eyeing the muscular, tapering back with a feeling that had she possessed a knife she might very well have been tempted to use it—except that it almost certainly would have bounced right back. Clay was invincible; too sure of himself, too aware of his power over her. And now Ian was to add to the complications. She would have given anything right then to be safely back in London with Barney. He was the only man who could offer her the kind of haven she needed.

Glenn was also looking after the receding figure as he came up. 'Wasn't that our Cruise Director?' he asked on an odd note.

'Yes.' Alex pushed her sunglasses further up her nose. 'He has to get back to the ship.'

'He's going away from the hotel.'

'Perhaps he's left his things further down the beach.' She looked up brightly. 'Did you manage to fix lunch?'

'Yes. They said about fifteen minutes.'

'Then I'd better go and change. I can hardly go into the restaurant in a bikini.' She came to her feet, gathering her scattered belongings. 'I'll see you in the foyer, shall I?'

If Glenn had thought anything of Clay's abrupt disappearance he made no further mention of it. At five they returned to the ship via the twisting coastal road which offered picture postcard views at every bend. The harbour at Charlotte Amalie was the loveliest of the whole cruise, best seen from the sea against the high green hills of the island's interior with the colourful town buildings stretching down to the water's edge. Alex had been on deck each of the three times the *Andromeda* had so far made this particular port while she had been aboard, and thought she would never tire of the long slow approach under the watchful eye of the great white citadel guarding the harbour entrance, of the sleek beauty of the slender-masted yachts riding the glassy blue surface of the water.

'It would be a marvellous place to have a house,' Glenn agreed when she made some such observation as they boarded. 'It's only five hours down from New York.'

It never failed to amaze Alex the way all Americans seemed to take flying as casually as getting into a car. A thousand miles was just a hop, the Caribbean a weekend retreat. Married to Glenn she would be able to go more or less anywhere in the world she wanted simply by expressing a wish. None of this saving up all year round for a fortnight's family holiday in some obscure resort for people in his bracket. It was a totally different world from the one in which she had been brought up, a different world from the one she had known these last three years, if it came to that. Yet was it the kind of life she wanted to lead? Her career aside, what exactly did she want?

It was at dinner that she saw Ian for the first time. He and his wife were sharing a table with Clay, but even from a distance it was apparent to Alex that their differences had not been in any way resolved. June looked flushed and mutinous, while from what she could see of Ian's face he was already wondering if following his wife all this way had been a good idea after all. She was glad he wasn't facing her way. What she had expected to feel on seeing him again she wasn't wholly certain, but she had expected something. Looking at him now was like looking at someone she had known a long time ago: he seemed so young, for one thing, his features almost boyish beneath the modishly long fair hair—and there was a certain weakness about his jaw she had never noted before. It didn't seem possible that there was the man who had driven her into running away from everything she held dear.

'You're very quiet,' Glenn said, and she came back to earth to find him watching her with that same odd expression he had worn earlier when he had found her with Clay. 'You've been quiet all afternoon.'

'I'm sorry.' She gave him an apologetic little smile. 'Carnival night is always a bit of a worry until it's over. It gets so hectic backstage.'

'Of course. I should have realised.' He sounded almost relieved. 'It's nice to think that I don't have to take my leave along with the rest in the morning. What would you like to do?'

Alex would have preferred to stay on board for once and just laze, if the truth were known, but with Ian around that was obviously not going to be a good idea. 'Perhaps we could go out to the Gold Coast,' she said, knowing he would readily agree to anything she suggested. That, at least, should be far enough away to preclude the possibility of running into Clay again. She looked across at the maturely handsome features of her companion and wondered why she kept hesitating. Glenn was all that most women could ask for in a man, and a great deal more than most women got. She might not be in love with him, but she was fond of him, and that kind of emotion could grow into love given the opportunity. So what was she waiting for?

After what she had said about the show, Glenn insisted that an early night would not go amiss. Alex put up no argument, glad to be alone in her cabin after the strain of the performance. Clay must have arranged for his party to have a table so close to the floor deliberately so that he could watch Ian's reactions when she came on. She had no idea what those reactions might have been because she had hardly dared to even glance in their direction, but just knowing they were all three there had been enough to undermine her concentration. The applause had been just as enthusiastic as on the previous nights, only she herself knew that she had not given of her best, and that fact alone was enough to upset her.

She was sight reading her way through a copy of an old blues number Jimmy Keen had loaned her when the gentle tap came on the door. Heart racing, she sat where she was for an indeterminate moment before getting up to move across.

'Who is it?' she asked, and felt an odd mixture of relief and dismay run through her at the answer.

'It's me, Ian.' His voice was low but audible through the wood. 'Alex, I must talk to you. Please!'

She opened the door, standing there looking at him with cool, unsmiling features. 'You must be mad coming down here like this,' she said. 'What do you want?'

'To explain ... and to apologise.' He looked miserable and hangdog. 'I've made a complete mess of things, haven't I?'

'It certainly seems that way.' Alex spoke chillingly, but he looked so wretched it was impossible to stop herself from softening a little. 'I don't really think there's much point in talking about anything. Especially not now at this time of night. You realise what your brother-in-law is going to think if he finds out you've been to see me?'

'Clay never thought much of me anyway. He'd probably be glad if June and I did break up.' He paused, looking beyond her into the cabin. 'Can I just come inside for a minute or two? If I don't talk to somebody about it I'll go round the bend!'

Her hesitation was brief. It was better for him to be inside with the door closed than standing out there in full view of anyone passing. 'You'll have to make it quick,' she agreed with reluctance.

'You must think me a real swine,' he said frankly when they were facing one another across the narrow expanse of carpet. 'I gathered from what June said that you hadn't let on about me not telling you about her before we finished. Thanks for that, Alex.'

'Don't mention it.' She couldn't resist a small edge of irony. 'As the other woman I was in line for most of the blame anyhow. Am I supposed to have seduced you too?'

'I never said *that*.'

'You wouldn't need to,' dryly. 'Who'd believe otherwise in the circumstances? No, the "I did wrong, but I was led astray" routine holds far more credibility, I have to give you that.' She shook her head at his attempt to speak, already regretting the digs. 'Forget it, Ian. Unfortunately none of it seems to have done much good.'

'No.' He stuck his hands in his pockets. 'June wants me to suffer some more before she forgives me. It sounds a rotten thing to say, but in a way she's almost enjoying all this ... having me chase out here after her.'

'Can you blame her?'

He looked up then. 'Don't you see, that's been half the trouble with us from the start. June never would try to see things realistically. I could never discuss any problems with her because she'd just say they'd sort themselves out if I'd only stop worrying ... either that or she'd suggest I asked Clay for advice. She still relies on him more than she ever did on me. Look at the way she came running to him over this.'

'And is he advising her?'

'I've no idea. She was on her own when I came aboard, and Clay didn't put in an appearance till gone six, so maybe he's decided to let us work things out for ourselves. Except that we don't seem to be getting anywhere. She would hardly speak to me at dinner. Needless to say we're not sharing a cabin. We're not even on the same deck.'

'Perhaps you're using the wrong tactics.' Alex eyed him steadily. 'Do you love her, Ian?'

'Yes.' The reply came without hesitation. 'That's why I made you out the villain of the piece. I thought if I told her the truth that would be the end. Not that it's made all that much difference.'

'Oh, I don't know. You're at least together again.'

'In the same boat?' with a quirk of humour. He leaned against the door and studied her a moment. 'What did you mean when you said I might be using the wrong tactics? What other kind *could* I use?'

His brother-in-law could probably have told him, Alex thought dryly, but Clay was apparently acting the part of observer this trip. 'Well, you've tried talking to her without getting anywhere, so maybe the situation calls for a little more action.'

'Such as?'

She gave a small impatient exclamation. 'Surely you don't need a blueprint? *Show* her how you feel, you dope! Kiss her!'

'I tried this afternoon. She wouldn't let me.'

June hadn't been all that wrong; he really did need Clay to advise him. 'Of course she wouldn't let you! She doesn't want to be asked, she wants to be shown.'

'Oh, come on! That dominant male thing went out with clubs and bearskins! The only way to deal with something like this is to reason it out.'

'You said she wasn't prepared to listen. Anyway, who told you that women were reasonable creatures?' Her voice sounded husky. 'We even fall in love for all the wrong reasons.'

'I'd have said in this American's case they were all the right ones.' He was looking at her curiously. 'According to what June told me, he's loaded.'

Alex attempted a smile. 'For someone who denies being able to even talk to his wife you seem to have covered quite a lot of ground in a few hours!'

'I suppose she was testing me. Trying to find out if I'd react.' He paused. 'Are you going to marry him, Alex?'

'I don't know. And it isn't me we're talking about.' She put up a hand and wearily pushed back her hair from her eyes. 'Ian, I can't tell you what to do ... nobody can. I've said what I think and if that's no good then you'll just have to play it the way you see it. One thing is certain, you shouldn't be here with me.'

'And that's as good a way as any of telling me to go.' He moved, to stand awkwardly with his hand on the doorknob for a moment. 'I had to see you alone like this, if only ...'

'If only to prove to yourself that I didn't mean anything to you?' she finished for him.

'Something like that, I suppose.' He glanced at her. 'If it's of any interest I still think you're the best companion anyone could have had.'

'Man's best friend.' The flippancy was strained. 'Goodnight, Ian. And good luck!'

'Thanks.' His answering smile was wry. 'I'm going to need it.'

It was more than luck she needed, Alex told herself as the door closed softly behind him. It was a good stiff dose of backbone to get her through the rest of this interminable voyage.

The proposed trip out to Puerto Rico's Gold Coast did not after all materialise. Going along to Glenn's suite in answer to a telephone summons Alex found him lying wanly in bed with the ship's doctor already in attendance.

'A spot of gastric trouble,' the latter assured her. 'Nothing to worry about, but best to stay in bed till it settles down. The heat out there will only make things worse.'

'Must have been that lobster we had at lunch yester-day that disagreed with me,' Glenn said ruefully when the medical officer had gone. 'I should have known bet-ter. I'm sorry about this, Alex. I should be fit enough by this afternoon, though. We could go out to Boca de Cangrejos. They say that at low tide you can walk right out to the coral caves.'

'You're not going anywhere today,' she stated firmly. 'The doctor said you were to stay in bed and I'm sure he was right. You look as though you didn't get much sleep last night.'

'No, I didn't.' It was obvious that he still didn't feel at all well. 'Are you sure you don't mind staying on board all day?'

'Of course not.' Alex stilled her faint sense of disquiet over the way in which he had taken it for granted that she would not be going anywhere without him. 'I'm way overdue with my correspondence anyway. This will give me a good opportunity to do some catching up.' She bent down and put her lips swiftly to his cheek. 'You stay there and catch up on some sleep. I'll look in again later.'

The decks were almost deserted at this hour. Alex went in to the restaurant and ate a light breakfast of fruit juice, scrambled egg and coffee, sitting alone at their table for two by one of the windows and idly viewing the comings and goings along the Wharf. The departing passengers had not yet begun to disembark, although she could see a growing pile of luggage be-yond the gangway waiting to be picked up and trans-ported to the airport. Before long that pile would have been replaced with another, this time to be taken on board for the incoming party. All it needed, she thought satirically, was for Sally to put in an appearance now and her cup would really be flowing over.

Someone slid into the seat opposite and she looked round to meet Marian Lee's sneering gaze.

'The millionaire run out on you? Shame! Never mind, there's plenty more fish in the sea.'

'For everyone,' Alex rejoined. She put down her coffee cup with care. This was the first time the dancer had attempted to speak to her since the night she had ripped up the black dress, and it was still too soon. 'What do you want?'

'From you?' The other laughed. 'That's the thousand-dollar question. What would you consider it worth for me to keep quiet about last night?'

Alex stiffened. 'What about last night?'

'You're asking me?' The jeer turned abruptly to calculation. 'Let's just say I was on my way to my cabin when I saw a certain gentleman heading in the direction of yours.'

'So you followed.'

'Naturally. I saw him go in and I didn't see him come out again. Enough said?'

Alex searched desperately for some route of escape and found none. Marian had seen Ian come to her cabin last night and she was going to make hay out of that knowledge if she could. It was hers and Ian's word against the dancer's, but who was going to believe them? If Marian went to June there would be no way of saving the Marriots' marriage. Knowing it wasn't going to be any good, she nevertheless tried to bluff her way out. 'What makes you think that's worth anything to keep quiet about?'

'The fact that the man in question just happens to be married to Clay Anderson's sister, that's what. I saw them together in the afternoon.'

'You seem to have eyes all over the place.' Alex paused momentarily. 'But I hardly think that qualifies you to recognise him again on a dimmed alleyway.'

'Don't try that one. If it wasn't Ian Marriot in your cabin last night, who was it?'

'Why not ask me?' The question was soft but deadly in its intonation, jerking both girls into awareness of a third party to their conversation. Clay had approached unseen and unheard behind a group even now taking their places at the next table down with chattering enthusiasm. He was in uniform and carrying his cap, but there was no duty smile on the grimly set mouth. Marian licked lips suddenly dry and attempted to regain control of the situation.

'All right then, I'm asking you.'

'And you've got your answer, for what's its worth.'

She stared at him, face slowly flushing with something more than just anger. 'That's a damned lie, and you know it!'

'Why should I lie?'

'To stop your sister getting to know about it, that's why. Well, it won't wash—I know who I saw going into that cabin, and it certainly wasn't you!'

'If two people swear that it was you can hardly prove them wrong.' His gaze switched to Alex, the message in them only too clear. 'Right?'

She nodded, unable to trust her voice, saw his jaw contract and forced an answer through stiff lips. 'That's right.'

Marian looked from one to the other of them, her

striking features set in vicious lines. 'You're not going to get away with it like that,' she said. 'I'll . . .'

'I think we are.' Clay had a smile on his face now for the benefit of the people on the lower table who were beginning to take an unwelcome interest in their little tableau. 'And while we're on the subject, you try telling my sister anything at all and I'll have you off this ship quicker than you can blink. Now get out of here!'

Marian went. Faced with that icy assurance, Alex felt she would have done the same thing in her shoes. Yet she was also sure that the other would not be content to leave it there. But that was something to be faced later. At present there was Clay to contend with. She looked at him in some desperation, uncaring of what the party next door might be thinking. 'Clay . . .'

'We'll go outside,' he said. He kept his voice low, the smile fixed.

Alex got to her feet and moved with him towards the restaurant doors. She even managed a smile for the bus boy carrying the fresh pot of coffee she had ordered some five minutes previously. 'Sorry, I decided not to bother.'

There was a great deal of activity out in the foyer, with people flowing both up and down the central stairway. Clay drew her out on deck and into one of the boat bays out of sight of the main doors.

'I'd like to throw you overboard,' he gritted. 'You *and* that brother-in-law of mine! You just couldn't wait to get together again, could you!'

Alex drew in a shaky breath, searching for the right words—if there were any right words. 'Before you start jumping to conclusions shouldn't you make sure of a few facts?'

'The only fact I'm interested in is that Ian was in

your cabin last night. Or are you going to try denying that too?'

'No, he was there. But not for the reason *you*'d naturally imagine.'

'I suppose he just came to talk?'

'As a matter of fact, that's exactly what he did do. His wife won't talk to him, and you're not the most approachable of people, so I was the obvious alternative as the only other person involved.'

'Involved is the word! I should have known he wouldn't be able to keep away from you. You're like a candle flame to a moth ... and just about as deadly!'

'Clay, you've got to listen to me.' She was trembling and trying her best not to let it show. 'Ian loves your sister, not me. He ...'

'That I've never doubted,' he cut in hardily. 'If he didn't he'd hardly have given you up for her. Being in love with one woman doesn't mean a man automatically stops wanting others, it means he makes some attempt not to put that need into practice. What he *doesn't* need is any encouragement to break the rules ... especially from someone like you.' His mouth had twisted. 'I couldn't come down too hard on him the first time, but he'd better find enough willpower to put you right out of his mind from now on or I'll take him apart! As for you ...' he stopped, jaw clenching ... 'if I thought beating the hell out of you would do any good I'd do it right here and now, but all I'd get out of that is a bit of personal satisfaction. What you need is a permanent bruise—the kind you couldn't forget—and I'm going to take a personal interest in seeing that you get it, one way or another!'

Alex could feel the rail at her back, as hard and unyielding as the man in front of her. It was like being in a trap, snared by a web of circumstances which could only be disproved by one person. And having lied in the first place Ian wasn't going to jeopardise his position still further by admitting it—especially after his brother-in-law got through with him. Why bother anyway? Clay's opinion of her was not going to be changed by anything Ian said. He'd probably put it down to an attempt on the other's part to stand by her. Pride came to her rescue, lifting her chin and hardening her eyes.

'Go to hell,' she said thickly. 'And take Ian with you! So far as I'm concerned the whole business never happened.'

She half expected him to stop her as she stepped round him and made for the door again, but he stayed where she had left him. Only when she reached the privacy—and safety—of her own cabin did she let her control relax, feeling the shakiness of her limbs without surprise. She had imagined that matters could get no worse, but she had been wrong. There had been a quality in Clay's anger that had not been there before, an urge to hurt which struck far deeper with her than any physical threat. He had made the whole issue personal from the start, but never quite to this extent.

One thing was certain, whatever form his retaliation took it would hit her where he imagined it would do most harm, and that indicated through Glenn. Only he was wrong, because whichever way the latter reacted to the story it would make little difference to her life. Glenn was kind and generous and understanding—all the things she had once thought so necessary in a man before love could evolve. But he wasn't the man she did love, and it was time to stop burying her head in the sand over that particular truth.

She stayed in the cabin for the rest of the morning,

somehow resisting the temptation to pour out her heart to Barney on paper. He had provided the means of escape from one incident; it was hardly fair to saddle him with the results. This was something she had to see through on her own the best way she could. And if she came out of it with the kind of heartache she anticipated then that too would have to be borne. Running away from what she had imagined she felt for Ian had served only to underline the fact that it was no solution to any problem. From now on she stayed put and faced up to things the way they were.

CHAPTER SEVEN

Going along to the suite after lunch, Alex found Glenn up and sitting in an armchair in his dressing-gown, although it was apparent that he still didn't feel wholly himself again yet.

She had contemplated beating Clay to it by telling him about Ian herself, but when faced with the prospect of introducing the subject in cold blood, as it were, found that she couldn't bring herself to start. Perhaps the best thing was to let someone else do the telling after all, and then use the subsequent explanations as a jumping-off point from which to sort out their own position. She hated the thought of Glenn being hurt by anything she had done, only whatever happened he was obviously going to be. Her only consolation was in the knowledge that a marriage between them could never

have worked out happily in any case, and no doubt
Glenn would realize that for himself eventually—as
Sally obviously already had. Regrettably that promised
future friendship with the younger girl would never
materialise now.

By dint of persuasion Glenn eventually agreed to stay
in the suite until early evening. Alex promised to meet
him in the Connaught Bar at seven providing he felt up
to it. She was grateful when he made no attempt to persuade her to stay longer, having already found the
effort of dissimulation almost more than she could cope
with over the last hour.

Despite the attractions offered ashore the Beach Deck
was fairly well populated by the time she reached it.
She found herself a quiet corner in which to concentrate on the letters she had neglected earlier, forcing a
note of breezy unconcern as she penned the words likely
to be expected from someone at present enjoying all
the delights of the Caribbean while others toiled in the
cold and wet of a British December.

It would be Christmas in less than three weeks, she
realised with a small sense of shock. Out here, with the
days so much alike, time ceased to have any real meaning, although she supposed the ports of call themselves
formed a calendar of sorts. Christmas week aboard the
Andromeda was reputed to be an experience not to be
missed. By that time the worst really should be over,
though it would still leave her with half her three
months to go.

The worst part would be in seeing Clay every day
with no possible chance of ever breaking through the
barriers between them. Loving him like this was probably illogical after all that had passed between them,
yet logic seemed to have little to do with emotion. He

had done what he thought was right in the face of the evidence against her, and she had to concede that it was pretty damning. The fact that it was all circumstantial meant nothing without proof to the contrary, and that she didn't have. Ian was the real culprit, yet even he had some excuse for behaving as he had. Calling at her cabin last night had been a crazy thing to do, but he had been fairly desperate. Anyway, it had only been one more nail in her coffin, and the ones already there had been more than enough to seal the lid of any chance of ever reaching Clay.

Leaving the desk at six she caught a glimpse of Philip Osbourne talking to a pretty redhead alongside the pool with some animation. Since Glenn's return to the ship the young officer had not tried to seek her out, apparently judging the competition too heavy for any further pursuit on his part. That was the trouble with men, she reflected wryly: their whole interest in women was centred in the physical. It was what made Barney so special to her. He was one of the very few men she had met who didn't look at her like a dog at a bone. *His* interest, thank goodness, lay in his pocket linings, with enough left over to extend un undemanding hand in friendship. If she was going to love anyone at all she would be safer sticking to someone like that. One might miss all the heights, but at least stay clear of the depths.

She got out clean underwear before going in to take a shower, leaving it ready on the chair for when she came out again. She was already under the water before she remembered that she hadn't put on the door catch, but there was no reason why the steward should take it into his head to come into the cabin at this time of the evening, so she decided it could safely be left. The warm

water was refreshing after the sticky heat of the afternoon. She let it play over her for several minutes, wish-
ing she had allowed herself enough time to wash her
hair. As she turned off the tap she thought she caught
the sound of movement from the outer cabin, but the
noise was not repeated and she continued to towel herself dry.

The confining cap had flattened her hair. She ran her
fingers through it to lift it again, then pulled on a
towelling robe, drawing the tie belt about her waist as
she opened the door to step through into the cabin.

Shock held her rigidly there in the doorway, one foot
poised to bridge the dividing strip, eyes fixed on the
man lounging in the bed with the top cover drawn
lightly over the lower half of his body and his bare
shoulders gleaming dull bronze in the dimmed radiance
of the reading light behind him. On the chair close by
lay slacks and a shirt, flung casually down to join but
not hide her own garments. A pair of shoes askew underneath completed the picture.

Even as she stood there frozen there came a brisk rap
on the outer door. Clay gave her a tautly mocking smile
and settled his weight comfortably on one elbow as he
called, 'Come in.'

Alex brought her head round slowly to see Glenn's
stunned gaze sweep over the scene, and draw the
natural conclusion. She couldn't find a word to say;
couldn't even find her voice. All she could do was watch
the pain take over from disbelief, that in its turn to be
superseded by bitter contempt.

'So it's true,' he said. 'Everything that woman told
me was the truth!' There was nothing of the man Alex
had known these past days in the look he slid over her.
'You've got more than just a voice to offer the media;

I'd say your acting ability was worth an Oscar any day of the week! Too bad you didn't take a little more care in other directions. Too bad for you; a lucky break for me.' His gaze moved briefly to Clay lying there listening without concern. 'She's all yours. I'll get off in La Guaira.'

It took the sharp closure of the door again to jerk Alex out of the state of suspended animation which had claimed her. Even then her mind refused to function properly. She felt totally at a loss; almost numb. When she looked across at Clay it wasn't with hatred; it wasn't with any kind of emotion at all.

'You knew he was coming here.'

'Yes.' He didn't move, watching her with an expression which held some element in addition to vindication. 'I saw Marian Lee leave his suite a few minutes ago and took a gamble that he'd be down here in short order to face you with what she'd told him. Finding you in the shower was a bonus.' His smile was unamused. 'Gave me time to arrange some props. I don't think you're going to find a way out of this one!'

She drew in a small shuddering breath as the numbness began to recede. 'Did you have to involve Glenn? What harm did *he* ever do you?'

'None at all. And I've done him a favour. Next time he might think twice before taking a shine to a woman half his age.' He shoved back the cover and swung his legs over the edge of the bed, reaching for his slacks. His eyes came back to hers as he stood up to pull them on over the dark blue briefs, expression sardonic. 'Now I know what partial amnesia must feel like.'

Alex still couldn't react; her legs were too shaky to support any sudden movement. There was an aching tightness in her chest and at the back of her eyes, but he wasn't going to see her break down. Not now. Not any time. She was going to keep the hurt locked inside her if it killed her—at least until he had gone.

Shirt in hand, he studied her with faint bafflement. 'Nothing to say?'

It took everything she had to answer him without letting her voice betray her. 'Nothing you'd understand. Can we call it a day now?'

'My God, you're hard!' He said it savagely, muscles tensing as his fingers curled into the material he was holding. 'You got it all when they were dishing it out, didn't you: face; body; voice—and a calculating——' He broke off, fingers relaxing to let the shirt slip through them to the floor. 'Well, there's one way of getting to you!'

'No!' She put up her hands involuntarily in front of her to fend him off, her whole body tensed against the bulkhead behind her. 'Don't you . . .'

That was as far as she got before he stopped her, pulling her hard against him and covering her mouth with his. Resistance was not only futile, it was inflammatory. Alex gave in because there was no other way out, letting the response come without fighting it and feeling the dampness on her cheeks below her closed lids. When he finally stopped to study her she made no move to turn her head away. She heard his small intake of breath, followed by a pause which seemed to stretch for an age before he said roughly, 'Now say it!'

There was to be no letting up; he was out to get his full pound of flesh. Alex made a faint motion with her head and felt her chin taken and held in a grip which made further movement impossible. '*Say* it!'

'I . . . don't know what you want me to say.' The words came painfully.

'You know.' His voice was low and unrelenting. 'Just three simple words—*I want you*. And you're going to say them, believe me. This is one time you're not going to wriggle off the hook. You'll say it now or you'll say it later, the choice is up to you. Only don't wait too long to make it or I'll make it for you—and I shan't be gentle about it either!' His hand jerked her chin. 'Look at me!'

She did, finding his eyes as granite-like as she had anticipated. What he was doing to her was in its own way worse than any physical retribution, stripping her of every last vestige of pride. Yet it was only the truth— or a part of the truth.

'I want you,' she said.

For a second or two he remained as he was, a muscle contracting sharply just below his cheekbone, then he let her go and stood back, bending to pick up his shirt. Alex watched him put it on and tuck it into the top of his slacks, slide his feet into his shoes. Only when he was fully dressed again did he glance her way, face tightly controlled.

'*Now* we can call it a day.'

She was still standing exactly as he had left her when the door closed behind him. There was finality in the sound.

Glenn left the ship the next morning. Alex didn't try to see him before he went; there seemed little point. Perhaps it was even kindest in the long run that it had happened the way it had. He was hurt and disillusioned now, but the pain would be briefer because of it. And he could always console himself with the knowledge of his lucky escape.

She took the pendant from the ship's safe later that morning and parcelled it carefully for return by regis-

tered post. One of the crew going ashore took care of
the posting for her. It cost a small fortune to cover the
registration fee, but once it was out of her hands she
felt better. Now she only had one thing to think about.

There had been a short time last night when she had
been on the verge of pleading indisposition to get out of
doing the show, but something stronger than herself
had refused to allow that depth of capitulation. She had
gone on as scheduled, donning a professional mask with
a facility which amazed her, thinking about it afterwards. Clay had not put in an appearance, but she was
sure he had been there somewhere. Switching her plan-
ned closing number for an old standard she had been
saving for Tuesday's performance had been purely instinctive. There was something particularly poignant
about a song like 'More Than You Know' at a time like
this. She had known as soon as she finished that she
would probably never sing it again, partly because she
could never top tonight's rendering and partly because
it would bring back too much she wanted to forget.

The week wore on. Alex was back at a table for four,
this time sharing with a family group of three. The
Benitos had emigrated to America from their native
Italy twenty years previously, and now owned a chain
of supermarkets. They had a daughter about to marry
the son of one of their hometown's prominent citizens,
and the son aged six who had accompanied them on
this trip south.

Alex took care of the boy on the Wednesday evening
while his parents went ashore to sample the Barbados
night life, switching to early dinner so they could have
it together. Afterwards she took him to the ship's
cinema for the first showing of that night's film. It was
a comedy of the mainly visual kind designed to appeal

to all nationalities. The dialogue was in English with Spanish subtitles. Sitting in the darkness of the tiny auditorium with the laughter practically lifting the deck above their heads, she managed to cast off depression for the first time in days. It was good to hear young Michael chuckle with glee at the antics on screen, to see him clutch his cheeks when Peter Sellers pulled off yet another of his beautifully timed gaffes.

She was still smiling when the lights went up and they got to their feet to leave, then she saw who had been sitting two rows behind them and felt the smile stiffen on her lips.

Clay had a hand on his sister's shoulder, urging her out into the aisle ahead of him to join the file making their way towards the exit. There was no sign of Ian. Even as she saw them Clay turned his head a little and spotted her, his glance dropping to the small figure at her side before coming back to her face with an unfathomable expression. Alex thought she knew what he must be thinking: someone like her had no right to be in charge of a child. She clutched Michael's hand a little tighter, causing him to look up at her.

'It's not bedtime yet?' he asked hopefully. 'Can we watch the cabaret?'

'I think not.' She hung back to let the people behind move ahead of them. 'Your mother said you were to be in bed by half past nine and it's almost that now. We'll get the steward to bring you a drink to the cabin.'

The other two had gone by the time they reached the foyer. They took the lift to Boat Deck where the Benitos had their stateroom, and Alex arranged the promised drink while Michael got ready for bed. She read him a story from *Brer Rabbit* while he was drinking his chocolate, taking the mug gently from him when his eyelids started to droop. When she left the cabin he was already fast asleep, curly head cherubic on the pillow.

It was still barely ten when she emerged on Connaught Deck from the lift. The cabaret was in full swing; she could hear the music used in one of the chorus routines. There was no point in spending the next half hour or so until it was time to check on Michael again mooching round the ship. She slipped into the club from the rear and found herself a spare seat, not realising who was standing nearby until Philip slid quietly into the chair next to her.

'Hi,' he murmured. 'First time I've seen you on your own in days.'

'Yes.' She scarcely knew what else to say. 'It seems a very full ship this week.'

'I'd have thought it would seem empty since La Guaira,' he came back meaningfully. There was a pause before he added in the same tones, 'Or was it you who gave *him* the push?'

He was talking about Glenn, of course. Odd how he had slipped into the rear of her memory these last few days. 'Does it have to be one or the other?' she asked. 'He had a job to get back to.'

'He booked an indefinite passage. Nobody does that and then changes their mind inside a few days. Not without a very good reason.'

She refused to meet his eyes. 'Perhaps he had one.'

'Clay?'

She looked at him then, heart constricting. 'Philip . . .'

'I know,' he said, 'it's none of my darn business, only . . .' the hesitation was brief . . . 'is it true that Freeman found the two of you together in your cabin?'

Shipboard grapevine, Alex thought painfully. Did

everyone know about that incident? She studied Philip's face in the semi-darkness, glad there was no one else close enough to overhear what was being said. She could try explaining the circumstances but she doubted if he would understand. Who could be expected to? And why bother anyway? If Philip harboured any doubts at all, wasn't it kindest in the long run to let him think of her as not worth losing any sleep over?

'Yes,' she said, 'it's true.' She got to her feet, resting her hand for a fleeting moment on his shoulder in passing. 'I'm sorry, Philip.'

So that was that, she thought heavily, making her way back towards the lifts. One disillusioned young man. Only he would get over it. She wished she could say the same for herself. This whole business had become more than she could cope with.

The alley was quiet as she went along to the Benitos' stateroom. Expectant as she was of finding Michael still soundly sleeping, it took her several seconds to adjust to the sight of the empty pillow on the pull-down berth. A quick search of the cabin and adjoining bathroom confirmed his absence. Panic grew inside her as her mind flashed over the many possibilities. If he had only been pretending to be asleep when she had left, he had had more than half an hour in which to get up to mischief. By now he could be anywhere. She thought of the open upper decks and controlled the sweeping fear with an effort. They were in harbour, yes, but there was still over forty feet of water out there. If Michael had climbed the rails on boat deck, for instance . . .

She clamped down there. It was hardly likely he would have gone outside when there was so much more of interest happening inside. He had said he wanted to see the cabaret. That was the place to start looking.

The Barbadian Police Band was in full spate when she arrived back on Connaught. Philip had gone from the small rear table they had shared so briefly. She stood for a moment in the doorway surveying the room and wondering where on earth to start. Michael's parents would be back at eleven at the latest, and if she hadn't found him by then she didn't know how she was going to face them.

'Lost something?' came sardonic tones from over her left shoulder. 'He left right after you did, if you've had second thoughts about staying.'

The irony barely registered as she acknowledged the need for help. If anyone could find Michael, Clay could.

'I've lost young Michael Benito,' she said desperately. 'I thought he might have come up here to see the band.'

He had come instantly alert. 'How long since you last saw him?'

'Thirty-five—forty minutes, no more. I—I thought he was asleep when I left him. He . . .'

'Save it,' he clipped. 'What time are you expecting his parents back?'

'Eleven, they said.'

'Then you'd better get back to the cabin in case they find it empty. I'll have an announcement put over the PA system, and call in the team.'

'The team?' she repeated stupidly, and saw his lips curl in impatience.

'We have a routine for this kind of thing. If you'd alerted the office from the cabin we could have had it in operation by now. Go on back down before the Benitos get back, will you.'

Alex went—there was nothing else she could do. She could see the sense in Clay's argument. Where was the use in one person wasting time looking over a ship the size of the *Andromeda* for a single small boy? With everyone alerted there was far more chance of his being spotted on the public decks, and the search team would cover those parts not normally accessible to the passengers. She had allowed panic to freeze common sense, and Clay was not going to let her forget it, that was for certain.

She had entertained faint hopes that Michael might have returned to the cabin during her absence, but it remained as empty as when she had left it. The announcement came over the public address system as she stood irresolutely in the middle of the floor. How long did it take to search a whole ship? An hour? Two hours? More? What was she going to say to the Benitos when they returned to an empty cabin? They had left Michael in her charge and she had failed them.

The following twenty minutes were some of the longest of Alex's life. When Clay finally appeared in the open doorway carrying the small, sleepy figure clad in pyjamas her relief was so great she almost snatched the child from his arms, hugging him to her.

'Michael darling, where have you been!' she demanded. 'You've had us all so worried!'

'Wanted to see Peter Sellers again,' came the murmur, and he struggled to free himself. 'Tired now.'

'He was at the back of the cinema on the floor fast asleep,' Clay volunteered as they both watched the boy climb between the sheets and drop almost at once into oblivion. 'He must have crept in after the second show started.'

Footsteps sounded along the alleyway outside before Alex could find anything to say, and the Benitos came quickly into the cabin, faces registering alarm.

'Somethins is wrong?' asked Michael's mother, eyes

switching from the sleeping face of her son to those of the other two occupants of the cabin. 'Michael has nightmare?'

Clay shrugged and smiled, deliberately making light of the event. 'He decided he wanted another look at the film he'd seen earlier with Miss Gaynor, then he fell asleep in the cinema. We just fetched him back.'

'Ah, the naughty boy!' She was more rueful than upset by the implications. 'We should never have left him, Tony. Always he gets into mischief.'

'*Si*,' her husband agreed without undue concern. 'But a boy is not a boy unless he seeks mischief. His smile at Alex held no trace of censure. 'You have been very good to us. Michael shall say he is sorry for troubling you in the morning.'

Somehow Alex found herself outside the cabin and moving along the alleyway at Clay's side. Only when they got to the foyer where the lifts were did she stop to lean against the nearest bulkhead and draw a breath of sheer overwhelming thankfulness.

'That was one of the worst hours of my life,' she said. 'Thank goodness it turned out all right!' She forced herself to look at the man standing there silently waiting, registering the expression on his face with sinking heart. 'I haven't thanked you for taking over the way you did. I'd never have found him in time.'

'You might never have found him at all,' he said. 'Not alive, at any rate. If you feel moved to play Lady Bountiful again any time, try confining your activities to those able to look after themselves.'

Anger and hurt mingled in just about equal amounts, making her uncaring of what she said. 'Like who, for instance? You? I can find better things to do with my time!'

'I'm sure you can.' His voice was dangerously soft. 'Only don't include young Philip in your plans.'

'Stop calling him that. He isn't a boy!'

'He's little more when it comes to dealing with some-one like you. You've got him tied up in knots, and I'm not going to stand by and see you tighten them any further for want of something better to do.'

She had come upright away from the hardness of the bulkhead, eyes dark. 'Meaning you'll find a way of dealing with the situation the same as you dealt with the last one? You mightn't find that so easy.'

'I think I might. Philip has principles you'd know little about. A word about Freeman's reasons for leaving the ship in such a hurry should be more than enough to turn him off.'

'He already knows Glenn's reasons,' she said. 'The whole *ship* knows Glenn's reasons!' There was bitterness in her tone. 'Pity you didn't stop to think about *your* reputation when you were so busy sinking mine!'

His laugh was without humour. 'Mine won't suffer any that you'd notice. That's one male bastion you're not going to breach in a hurry.'

'Your sister might not agree with you.'

Grey eyes narrowed. 'Does that mean you might be thinking of telling her?'

The anger and need to lash back at him died to-gether, leaving her suddenly sickened. She shook her head wearily. 'No, it doesn't. It wouldn't be true any-way. Hasn't this whole thing gone far enough as it is?'

'Not while my sister and her husband are still kept apart by it.'

'Perhaps that's as much your fault as mine.'

'*My* fault?'

'Yes.' She tried to keep her voice level. 'June has

your kind of mentality when it comes to meeting someone halfway. Ian has to make all the concessions, it
seems. Isn't *he* entitled to any pride?'

He had come a step closer, eyes signalling a warning.
'About as entitled as you are to yours.'

'Clay, don't.' She tried desperately to avoid him.
'Someone might come!'

'So what? You just got through saying the whole
ship knows about us.'

'Crew, not passengers.' His hands were hard at her
back, his mouth too close for comfort. If he kissed her
now, no matter how harshly, she wouldn't be able to
fight him. She was through fighting anybody. 'There's
the Line's reputation to think about,' she tagged on,
and knew she had won when his hold on her slackened.

'You're right,' he said. 'It isn't worth it.' Lips twisting, he studied her rigidly controlled features for another brief moment, then he stepped back from her
with a satirically sketched salute. 'We'll wait for a more
private moment.'

Alex watched him out of sight around the first bend
in the stairs before forcing herself to move. Was he ever
going to let it finish?

CHAPTER EIGHT

SATURDAY and San Juan brought the usual change-over of passengers, the newcomers easily picked out by the relative pallor of their skins, where race did not make this means of identification irrelevant. By Sunday afternoon, with a whole night and morning at sea behind them, most were beginning to relax into proper holiday mood, the various groups on the sun decks gradually merging at the edges.

Unready to mingle, Alex found herself a corner of the upper deck where she could think her own thoughts in solitude for the time being. It was here that Ian came across her halfway through the afternoon. He looked so miserable she hadn't the heart to turn him away when he asked if he could join her, despite the knowledge of what Clay would have to say should he see them together.

'Things no better?' she asked softly when he showed no signs of cheering up.

He shook his head. 'I don't think they're ever going to be. I can't seem to get through to June at all.' There was a pause before he went on. 'Trouble is I should be getting back. I only took a week's leave of absence, and I've already overstayed that. I don't want to lose my job on top of everything else.'

'You can always get another job,' Alex pointed out mildly, and saw a faint wry smile cross his features.

'Not that easily. I only got this one because of my connections with Clay.'

Her throat constricted as it always did at the mention of that name. 'Does he have that much pulling power?'

'Naturally. Perhaps that's been half the trouble. I should have held out for the job I already had, even if it didn't pay the kind of money I needed to keep June in the manner she's accustomed to. I took the easy way because I was scared of losing her. I don't suppose it was giving her much of a chance to prove just how much she did feel for me.'

Alex was bewildered. 'You said the manner she's accustomed to,' she put in hesitantly. 'Surely that can't be so very far above what you could offer her on a normal salary? I mean, Clay has an excellent job, but it can't have provided such a high standard of living for two of them over the years.'

It was Ian's turn to look surprised. 'You mean you didn't know?'

'Know what?'

'That Clay *is* the Connaught Line—the greater part of it, at any rate.'

She stared at him, scarcely believing. 'I don't understand. If that's true, why is he here on board doing the job he's doing?'

'Ask me another. As a B.A. you'd think he'd need something a bit more challenging. Could be he just likes organising.'

'As he's organised you and June while you've been married?'

'And before.' He caught her eye and looked faintly sheepish. 'Well, all right, so I suppose I've tended to sit back and let him get on with it at times. It seemed a doddle initially.'

Alex said softly, 'But it didn't instill any respect for you in June.'

'Obviously not. She's always turned to Clay; I expect she always will turn to him now.'

'I think that's up to you.' Alex was still trying to come to grips with the new, overwhelming information and finding it difficult. She consciously brought her mind back to bear on the man at her side. 'I'd agree with what you've been saying. You have to prove to June that you're capable of standing on your own two feet without help from your brother, then she might start seeing you as something more than a figurehead.'

His wince was genuine. 'It's one thing to say it, another to hear somebody else. And to think I was drawn to you in the first place because you boosted my ego!'

'And that's all you were looking for.' It was a statement, not a question.

'I suppose it must have been.' He was silent for a moment. 'Sorry if I messed up your life at all.'

'No harm done.' Not for anything was she going to let him guess the extent of the damage. She veered abruptly away from that particular subject. 'Where is June now?'

'In her cabin. She had some letters to write.' His face took on an indecisive look. 'Do you think I should try again while I've got the chance?'

But Alex had had enough. She pushed herself upright, swinging her legs over the edge of the lounger and reaching for her culottes. '*You* decide. I'm going down for some tea.'

Afternoon tea was served every day between four and four-thirty in the larger of the two saloon bars, with entertainment provided by a duo from the crew who played guitars and sang pleasant harmonies. Alex found a table for two close by one of the ports, and smilingly accepted a slab of fruit cake from the tray presented by a waiter, to go with her tea. It was going on for four-twenty and the place was almost full. When someone stopped beside her table and asked if she minded sharing, she shook her head, catching the waiter's eye for service before paying much attention to her new companion.

The woman was perhaps in her early fifties, blue-rinsed and expertly made up, with an expensively groomed look about her white linen dress and navy-blue jacket. Her face had once been piquantly pretty; it still was attractive despite the fine tracery of lines about mouth and eyes. She smiled in a typically friendly fashion.

'Hi there. I'm Eva Benson from Miami. You're Alex Gaynor, aren't you? I saw your photographs as we came aboard yesterday. You're singing tonight?'

Alex nodded and smiled back. 'That's right. Are you travelling alone?'

'Yes.' Just for a second something flickered in the shrewd, intelligent eyes. 'I met my second husband on one of these voyages, so every year I make the same old pilgrimage in the hope of picking up another. Not that I really expect to—there was only one Wally.' She paused, surveying Alex's face and hair with open appraisement. 'Do they offer you protection along with the fee? With those looks you must have the whole male crew foaming at the mouth.'

Alex had to laugh. 'Not that I've noticed. I'm just one of a crowd.'

'Hardly. As an entertainer you'd stand out even if you looked like the back end of a trolley-car.' Her tone was matter-of-fact, almost businesslike. 'What kind of stuff do you sing?'

'Rhythm and blues; some ballads.'

'Soul?'

Green eyes met blue-grey blandly. 'It was still there

last time I looked.'

This time it was the American woman's turn to laugh. 'I like you,' she said. 'You can stand up for yourself, if nothing else.'

'I can sing too.'

'As to that, I'll reserve my opinion. I've been sailing the seven seas too long to take it for granted that shipboard entertainment has to be top class. Half the acts out here couldn't make it back home.'

'Including those used by the Connaught Line?'

'Oh, they're not beyond coming up with a second-rater. Really good vocal chords don't often go with outstanding good looks—something to do with redressing the balance, I shouldn't wonder.' She paused, brows lifting in ironical inquiry. 'No offence meant, of course.'

'None taken.' Alex spoke the truth. Blunt as this woman was, there was nothing personal in her remarks. She was simply stating facts as she saw them, and she seemed to see them with remarkable clarity. 'I'll look forward to your verdict after tonight.'

The beautifully painted mouth widened again briefly. 'Puts you on your mettle, does it? That's good. Never had any time for those who go to pieces under fire.'

'Nobody could accuse our vocalist of that,' said Clay, stepping into view from somewhere behind Alex. He didn't look at her, his attention fixed on her companion, a smile of a different nature creasing his lips. 'Good to see you again, Mrs Benson. Sorry I wasn't here last night. I took a party ashore.'

'Wish I'd known, I'd have joined you,' returned the American woman easily. 'Where did you go—the Tropicoro?'

'Where else does a cruise party go in San Juan? I've

organised a night out when we reach Barbados this trip. Perhaps you'd like to join us then?'

'Sounds right up my street.' Her glance came back to Alex. 'Will you be going too?'

'Miss Gaynor has other commitments,' Clay put in before she could answer. 'She likes baby-sitting, among other things.' His change of tone was slight but noticeable to anyone looking for it. 'Hope you didn't get too much sun this afternoon. That was a bad spot to choose.' He gave Eva another of his pleasant smiles and moved on, back broad and powerful in the sparkling white uniform.

Alex brought her eyes up to meet a frankly speculative gaze.

'What goes on between you and our handsome Cruise Director?' Eva Benson asked. 'I sense conflict.'

The shrug was an effort. 'We don't hit it off.'

'A blind, deaf mute could guess that.' One beringed hand came up in sudden quick refutal. 'So it's none of my business. Never could keep my nose out of other folks' affairs.' Her grin was faint. 'Guess they're always that much more interesting than my own!'

Alex could conjure no resentment. There was something about the other which belied her apparent brittleness. 'It's a long story,' she said, knowing it more than possible that she would hear some of it during the week ahead. 'Did you want some more tea, Mrs Benson?'

'No, thanks, I only drink the stuff to be sociable. And the name is Eva.' The hesitation was brief enough to be almost non-existent. 'I noticed you're on a table for two in the restaurant. Any particular reason?'

'None, except that it's too much trouble to change.' Alex saw no call to explain why she had taken it in the first place. Without really thinking about it, she found herself responding to the faint appeal that had been in the question. 'Perhaps we could share, if you don't like the one you're at now?'

'Nothing wrong with the table but a couple of hypochondriacs I can do without.' She inclined her head. 'Thanks. This way I know what I'm getting.'

'On closer acquaintance you might not think it such a good move.'

'I'll risk it. I can always move again later in the week. What time are you on tonight?'

'Ten.'

'Then I shan't bother going in before that.'

Alex lifted her brows in faithful representation of the other's own gesture a few moments before. 'Don't you want to see the rest of the cabaret?'

'Dancers are a dime a dozen, honey, and magicians leave me cold.'

'This one wouldn't. He's special.'

'I'll take your word for it.' She pushed back her chair and stood up, the movement full of nervous energy. 'Meantime, I'm for my cabin—duty cards to write. If I don't get them posted in La Guaira tomorrow I'll be back before they get there. See you at breakfast—shan't be able to arrange the swap before that.'

Mealtimes from now on would be entertaining if not always relaxing, Alex conceded in some amusement as she departed. Eva Benson was a woman of strong opinions and didn't mind airing them. She felt a tinge of apprehension concerning that evening's performance, quickly squashed. Strong opinions didn't necessarily mean good judgement. If Mrs Benson didn't like her she would say so and that was as far as it would go. The time to worry was when nobody liked her. For the present, it was something to have a distraction from deeper problems.

Distractions came thick and fast that evening, starting with a fault in the PA system the ship's electricians couldn't seem to trace. With both microphones emitting weird whistles and screeches from time to time when they were working at all, entertainment promised to be somewhat erratic at its best. Alex breathed a sigh of relief when told at nine that all appeared to be in order again, disregarding the vagueness of the assurance because she didn't want to think of the possibilities of further failure. The clubroom was large, the acoustics not the best she had encountered. Without a microphone, any singer would be hard put to reach all parts of the audience.

Kreenia got through his act without cause for concern, although it would not have worried him overmuch had the system gone out again, as his act was mainly visual. Alex did one song, and had just started on another when without any warning whatsoever the mike faded on her. Finishing the fast, up-beat number without proper volume took some doing, but she did it to sympathetic applause. She could have opted out of the rest of the act without censure under the circumstances, only that was too much like admitting easy defeat. Instead she changed her programme, going for the straight, ballad-type songs which relied on voice rather than volume, bringing every ounce of technique she had to bear on projecting the notes to reach all parts of the clubroom.

The applause when she came off was deafening. The cabaret might not have been all it was supposed to be, but nobody seemed disposed towards complaint. Tired and dispirited, Alex changed in her dressing room to the white dress she had worn to dinner. An early night seemed a good idea if a dull one. There was nothing to stay up for anyway.

A tap on the door heralded the delivery of a message from Eva Benson inviting her to join her at a table in the bar which overlooked the club. Alex toyed with the idea of sending her regrets and pleading tiredness, then she shrugged and decided to accept. Might as well get it over.

The table to which the bar manager directed her on asking was set behind a pillar. It was only when she rounded it that she became aware of a third chair, already occupied by the last person she felt like facing tonight. Eva Benson looked anything but penitent.

'Congratulations,' she said. 'That was some performance. You're a real pro, girl!'

'Thank you.' Despite everything Alex couldn't help but feel gratified. She met Clay's glance with new heart, refusing to let her reactions show. 'I didn't realise it was to be a party.'

'Neither did I,' he said without expression. He looked back at Eva. 'Mind if I leave you two to celebrate alone?'

'Yes, I do,' she said firmly. 'As a ship's officer it's your bounden duty to keep an old customer happy.' She patted Alex's arm, eyes glinting with a humour not entirely without malice. 'Have some champagne and forget the war. It's a good vintage. You'll enjoy it.'

'I'm afraid I wouldn't know the difference,' Alex replied, watching the waiter pour her a glass. She longed to be anywhere but here with Clay sitting right next to her looking so grim. He had seen her with Ian this afternoon, and that hadn't helped. Darn Ian, she thought wearily. Darn all of them! Why couldn't they leave her alone?

'What exactly *are* we celebrating?' she heard herself asking. 'You must have ordered this before you knew whether I was going to be worth it or not.'

'It's my birthday,' came the response. 'And my third cruise aboard the *Andromeda* since Wally went. That reason enough?' Her voice had gone a little brittle. 'You know, you two remind me of a couple I once knew back in Chicago. They finished up married.'

It was Clay who answered, his eyes on the flush rising under Alex's skin with sardonic intent. 'Not, I imagine, to each other.'

Eva gave a short bark of laughter. 'You're a damned cynic, you know that? Take the girl to dance and straighten it out. I'll be here when you get back.'

There was a moment when he didn't appear to be going to move, then slowly he stood up, face clear of all but polite inquiry. 'Shall we?'

Alex could have refused, but she didn't think he was going to let her. Eva had been right about one thing, she thought numbly as they descended the wide staircase to the dance floor: she *couldn't* keep her nose out of other people's affairs. This wasn't going to help anything. Nothing could.

There were enough people already on the floor to make dancing apart fairly impossible. Clay made no attempt, pulling her in to him and bringing her hand down to rest against his chest.

'Try to look as if you're enjoying it,' he said close to her ear. 'You don't want the grapevine spreading more rumours, do you?'

'The ones already spread worry me more.'

'Why? Because of your precious reputation? Seems to me that went by the board some time ago.'

'I'm sure it would.' She was stiff in his arms, features rigidly composed. 'All right, we've danced, now can we go back? Eva can't work miracles.'

'Eva can, as well you know.' He made no effort to release her. 'That was a very astute move on your part. How did you manage it? She isn't usually open to an approach.'

'I don't know what you're talking about,' she came back coldly. 'If it's of any interest, she approached me, not the other way round. Am I supposed to know who she is?'

'If you don't you're losing your grip.' He paused and studied her face, his own changing expression a fraction. 'Ever heard of the Benson chain?'

Her heart did a painful double beat and settled again. Of course she had heard of it—everybody in show business had heard of it. Benson was a top night-club name in no fewer than six major cities across the States. Anyone booked to appear in one was assured of consecutive bookings in all five of the others—four months' work, at least, with plenty more to follow on the circuits. And Eva was Wallace Benson's widow: the woman who had the run the clubs for the last two years since his death, and without any fall-off in profits.

'I didn't connect it,' she said. 'You can believe it or not, but I simply didn't connect the name.'

His shrug was indifferent. 'I don't suppose it matters one way or the other. I'd say you were pretty sure of an offer before the week is up. Think you'll like the States?'

'How can I tell till I get there?' She wanted desperately to convince him of her lack of calculation, but saw no way to do it. '*If* I get there. Are you going to find some way to put a spoke in this wheel too?'

'Wouldn't work,' he said. 'So far as Eva Benson will be concerned, you could be carrying on with half the men on the ship so long as you can give her what she demands from an artist.'

'Pity you couldn't take a leaf from her book.'

'My involvement was personal, remember?' he came back with a warning glint. 'It still is. I told you to leave Ian alone.'

'We talked, that's all. You treat him like some kind of outcast, and your sister won't even let him through the door of her cabin. What do you expect him to do?'

'I expect him,' he said through his teeth, 'to keep his problems in the family! If he were half a man he wouldn't need advice on how to handle her!'

'Unfortunately he doesn't appear to have your know-how with women. Lack of experience, would you say?'

The music came to a stop. Clay looked at her for a long hard moment before abruptly letting her go. 'Let's get back,' he said.

Eva watched them coming, expression assessing. 'Enjoy yourselves?' she asked.

'Sure.' Clay drew out Alex's chair and saw her seated, but made no attempt to regain his own. 'Sorry I can't stay,' he said. 'Duty calls. Thanks for the champagne, Eva.'

'You're welcome. We must have some more before I leave. All three of us,' she added with deliberation.

There was a long moment of silence after he had gone. Alex toyed with her glass, conscious of the other's gaze on her bent head.

'You're in love with that guy, aren't you,' Eva stated. 'And he with you, if I'm not mistaken. So where's the problem?'

'You're mistaken.' Alex could suddenly stand no more. She pushed back her chair and came to her feet again, limbs shaky. She might be throwing away the chance of a lifetime by doing this, but she had to get away. 'Excuse me,' she said. 'I need some fresh air.'

She took the lift to Boat Deck, emerging into the open to find this starboard side of the ship deserted but for a couple leaning together against the rail some distance for'ard. Alex moved aft to find a canvas chair in one of the boat bays, letting the fitful breeze coming off the water lift her hair at the temples. It was a calm night, the waves long and smooth with scarcely any white tops to break the silver-dappled darkness. Somewhere up ahead beyond the far horizon lay the Venezuelan coastline and La Guaira. Already she was losing count of the number of times they had called there. She seemed to have been circling this sea for months rather than mere weeks.

Another couple came out through the same door she had used and turned in her direction. By the time she realised who they were it was too late to get up and move away without being seen. In any case, there was nowhere else to go this end of the deck.

Alex turned her face resolutely seaward and waited for the Marriots to pass, only to realise that they had stopped in the bay before the one she was occupying. Their voices were low, but even so it was apparent that they were arguing. June was shaking her head to whatever Ian was saying to her at the moment, her whole demeanour stubborn. He stood there looking at her for a moment, then suddenly he was striding off back the way they had come, vanishing inside the ship again and leaving his young wife alone.

Out of the corner of her eye, Alex saw June move further into the bay to lean her arms along the rail and look down into the darkness below. She looked as if she might be crying. For the moment there was nothing to be done but sit here and wait until the other girl decided to follow her husband inside. Ian, it appeared, was still trying to reason with her, and it still wasn't working. She felt sorry for them both, but there was nothing she could do to help.

The sudden terrified cry brought her jerking upright in her seat, nerves jangling. She had a brief glimpse of some object falling away from the side of the ship and vanishing. Where June had been standing bare moments ago there was now only emptiness.

Alex was on her feet and tugging free the nearest lifebelt from its moorings with a strength born of desperation, to heave it overboard. She had a vague impression of someone running towards her as she kicked off her sandals and clambered over the rail. Mind blank, body functioning like an automaton, she poised for a split second before launching herself out into space.

She seemed to fall in slow motion, the flimsy material of her dress flattened to her body. The impact was shattering, the force of it sending her shooting down into the dark depths until she thought she would never come up again. When she did break surface, winded and gasping for breath, it was to see the hull gliding past some yards away with a speed that shocked her. She struck out away from it, feeling the long skirt of her dress close about her legs like a shroud, dragging her down. The lifebelt wasn't far away, gleaming white as it moved with the waves, but it took her all her time to reach it.

Grasping it thankfully, she levered herself a little way up in the water to look for some sign of June. And there she was, a pale blur sliding down the side of a shallow wave not fifty feet ahead, arms moving feebly. Half paddling, half swimming with the lifebelt in tow, Alex finally managed to reach her, desperately fighting the encumbering folds of material swathing her legs. The other girl was barely conscious, her face an ashen mask apart from the gash at her temple. Fuller skirted than Alex's own, her dress had retained enough buoyancy to keep her afloat for those few precious extra moments.

Alex caught her under the armpits with one arm and held on grimly to the lifebelt with the other, knowing she could never summon the strength to get her inside it. Already the ship was far enough away for its full height to show against the sky, its stern lights gleaming indifferently down at them. It didn't even appear to be slowing, she thought, and fought for control against panic. That couple on deck must have seen the whole thing; of course they would be rescued! Only please God make them hurry, because her arm was turning numb with June's weight, her fingers slipping on the wet skin, the pain spreading into the muscles of her shoulder like tongues of fire.

She took in water as June made a sudden threshing motion of her limbs and went under, coming up retching and coughing, with fear no longer capable of being held in check. They were going to die out here, the two of them. They were going to drown. If it occurred to her at all that by letting June go she could save herself the thought was never allowed to gain ground. Her muscles had set until it was doubtful if she could have let go, her mind slipping numbly towards oblivion as they floated there beneath the cold hard light of the stars.

How long it was before the boat finally found them, she never knew. Sky and sea had merged into one overall blackness when she heard the faint, far-off splashing sounds. June's weight was taken from her arms and drawn upwards, then hands came under her own armpits and she was dragged from the water over the gunwales of the boat and laid along a seat. Blankets enfolded her, voices offered reassurance. She had a glimpse of somebody in white bending over June's body on the opposite side of the boat, then he was straightening and stepping across to where she lay, pushing back the soaked strands of hair from her face with a hand gentler than it had ever been in the whole fraught time of their acquaintance.

'How do you feel?' he asked.

'Sick,' she said, and was surprised at the strength of her own voice. 'Is June going to be all right?'

'Apart from a possible concussion, she's fine. Thanks to you.' He sounded gruff, his face taut with strain. 'Don't try to talk; there'll be time for that later.'

Reaction seized her suddenly in a fit of shivering she couldn't control. Things became something of a blur again, during which she was vaguely aware of reaching the ship and being hoisted aboard, of finding herself sitting in one of the loungers dragged hastily forward by somebody among the crowd of onlookers gathered to watch the drama, with June in another alongside. And then suddenly Ian was there, dropping to his knees at his wife's side with an anguished endearment that left no doubt of his feelings. June clung to him weakly, still too dazed to take in very much of what was happening but obviously glad of familiar arms.

The arrival of stretchers born by members of the crew broke up the crowd a little. Vaguely Alex heard someone telling somebody else about the incident, describing the way she had gone in after the other girl. When the stretcher-bearers came to take her she shook her head, pushing herself unsteadily to her feet.

'I'm all right,' she said. 'I'd rather just go down to my cabin and dry off.'

'I'll see to her, Jeff.' Clay moved forward into her line of vision. 'I think my sister's the only one who needs medical attention.' He took agreement for granted, stepping between them to swing Alex up against his chest regardless of the moisture still dripping from her.

'Clear a way there,' he crisply ordered those still thronging the deck. 'It's all over now.'

They were inside and making for the lifts before Alex could find enough spunk to protest. 'I can walk,' she said gruffly. 'Put me down, Clay, I'd rather walk!'

'I know.' His own voice was rough, his face set in lines she did not recognise. 'You'd rather do anything than let me touch you.' He glanced down at her then, eyes dark. 'Don't fight me, Alex. It isn't the time.'

It took them just three minutes to reach the blessed privacy of her cabin. When he finally set her down on her feet again she was shaking with more than just shock.

She didn't say a word when he took the blanket away from her, nor when he helped her out of the clinging ruin of her dress. She went with him unresistingly to the bathroom and watched him turn on the shower, leaning against the tiles with a mind gone blank of any kind of feeling at all.

'Stay under there at least five minutes,' he said. 'It will help calm your nerves. A bath would have been better, but beggars can't be choosers. I'll be right outside if you start feeling groggy. Shock can do odd things to the system.'

So could gentleness, Alex thought, when it came from unexpected quarters. She nodded without speaking, unable to find any words. When the door closed she got out of the rest of her things and stepped under the spray of fresh water, standing there until the trembling began to go from her limbs.

Clay was sitting in the chair when she eventually went back into the cabin. He looked at her for a long moment without saying anything, taking in the pallor of her face above the white towelling of her robe.

'Your hair's still dripping,' he said, and got up. 'Is there a dry towel?'

There was. He came out again with it in his hands and pressed her to a seat on the bed edge, kneeling behind her to take the ends of her hair between the two thicknesses of towel and rub out the excess moisture. Alex didn't move a muscle until he had finished, sitting stiffly upright with her hands clasped tightly in her lap.

'That should do it,' he said at last, and dropped the damp towel on the floor. In the following pause she could feel his gaze on her bent neck, then he got up again abruptly and moved away from her to lean against the dressing table. 'Can we talk about what happened up there, or would you rather be left alone?'

She shook her head numbly. 'I'm not all that sure what did happen. One minute she was standing there at the rail, the next she'd gone over.'

'Where were you at the time?'

'A little way along the deck. I don't think they knew I was there.'

'They?'

'Ian was with her at first. They were having a row, I think, and he left her. She ...' Alex stopped and looked up at him with distress in her eyes ... 'You're not thinking she might ... You don't really believe she could have jumped deliberately?'

He lifted his shoulders, face drawn. 'I don't know what to think. Her scarf was caught up on a spur of metal. It might have snagged there as she fell, or she might have been reaching for it. Only June can say for certain. She's been miserable enough over this business to make it a possibility. I've tried to talk sense into her, but she won't believe Ian cares enough. Maybe seeing the way he looked out there just now will convince her.'

'It should.' Alex hesitated. 'Clay, I'm sure she wouldn't have intended to go over. She must have been reaching for her scarf.'

'Risking her life for a bit of material?'

'Women are like that. And she mightn't have seen the risk. She was upset and didn't think.'

'But you did. You thought very quickly. That young couple who saw you go in after her said you were over the side before they could reach the spot.' He paused, made a small motion of his head. 'There's no adequate way of saying thanks for a thing like this.'

'Then don't say it.' They were under way again; she could feel the throbbing of the engines running through the plates beneath her feet. She didn't look at him. 'If I'd stopped to think I wouldn't have done it, so don't credit me with any heroics. Shouldn't you go and see how she is?'

'Yes, I suppose so. They've had time to assess the damage by now.' He straightened, his glance resting on her. 'You'd be better in bed yourself. You look all in. Will you go when I've left?'

'Yes.' Her voice sounded dull and strange; she knew tears lurked not so very far away. 'Thank you for bringing me down, although ...'

'I know. You could have walked on your own two feet.' His smile was strained. 'I'll have a couple of tranquillisers brought down, and you're to take them. Will you promise?'

She nodded, the lump in her throat making speech impossible. Head bent, she heard him move towards the door, heard him stop and make some sudden small exclamation under his breath, and then, unbelievably, he was coming back, lifting her to her feet and pulling her to him to press his cheek against hers and hold her.

'It's no use,' he said in low rough tones. 'It was bad enough before all this, but now ...' He broke off, arms loosening a little but not letting go of her. 'There has to be some way we can sort it all out. Maybe if we started over again somewhere else. It won't be easy, God knows, but at least we can try.'

'Clay ...' She was dazed and confused, unable to take in what he was saying in any way that made sense. 'I don't ...'

'You do. You want me the same way I want you. It's been there between us from the start.' He held her just far enough away from him to see her face, his own tensed so that the skin seemed stretched over his cheekbones. 'I saw the woman who'd ruined my kid sister's marriage walk into that Club and it was like being kicked in the stomach. Ironical, isn't it?'

'Is it?' Her voice was husky. 'I'd have said unfortunate. And how is tonight supposed to make any difference? I'm still the same person. You can't get involved with me without hurting June even more than she has been hurt.' She pushed herself free of him, eyes overbright, mouth stiff. 'And I'm not available that way. Not to you or to anyone else. I never have been. I know you don't believe it, but I can't help that.'

He studied her long and hard. 'You admitted to June that you'd gone after Ian. Why would you do that if it wasn't true?'

'Because ...' She shook her head hopelessly. 'It's no use. It's all too complicated. You wouldn't understand.'

'Try me.' He took hold of her hands, making her stay there in front of him. 'Tell me it all. From the beginning.'

'I can't.'

'Why?' His eyes narrowed. 'Because of Ian? Because you can show him for a liar as well as a cheat?' He assessed her reactions with a thin-lipped smile. 'Alex, you can't tell me anything about him that's going to surprise me too much. And what there is about this that I don't know already then I darn well want to know! Now tell me!'

It was difficult to start, but it got easier as she went along. She tried to tell it fairly to herself and yet find some mitigation for Ian, although from the way Clay was beginning to look about the mouth she was failing to convince him on that point. He stood there for a long moment in silence when she had finished, his ex-

pression mingling anger and self-recrimination in just
about equal amounts.

'I'd like to punch that weak-kneed little . . .' he began,
and broke off, jaw clenching. 'How June can feel like
she does about a man like that beats me hollow!'

'Perhaps she just doesn't see him the way you do,'
Alex said it softly, still uncertain of her own showing
in his estimation. 'If women only fell in love with men
who were everything they should be we'd never fall in
love at all. All Ian needs is to be made to feel that he's
more important to her than you are. He only lied in the
first place because he was scared stiff of losing her altogether.'

'He might do that anyway, because he's going to tell
her the truth if I have to stand over him while he does
it! When I think what he's caused . . .'

'Not just Ian. We all contributed a little initially,
didn't we?' She managed a faint smile. 'If I hadn't been
so pigheaded that first night we might have been able
to sort it out there and then.' The smile faded. 'Why
should he need to tell her anything? It isn't going to
make any difference to anybody now.'

'It's going to make a world of difference to us, and
I'm past thinking about anyone else right now. We're
going to sort out this mess from the bottom up, and
from there on in those two will have to do it on their
own. All that I'm interested in is clearing you of blame
in June's eyes, and if that means Ian has to carry the
can that's just too bad. It's time he got himself some
backbone.'

'Clay.' She spoke as evenly as she could. 'I meant
what I said. I'm not available on your kind of terms.'

'What kind of terms do you think I'm offering?' He
said it softly, but with an inflection which drew her

eyes to him. 'Why do you think I've been the kind of swine I have been the last few weeks? It wasn't all for June, believe me. It was my way of getting back at you for not being what I wanted you to be. You wait years for the right woman to come along, and when she does it turns out to be one you're supposed to despise. Do you know what it was like watching you with Freeman ... seeing him paw you around?'

'He never pawed me!'

'You know what I mean. That thing with Ian was just the excuse I needed to step in and finish it for good. All right, whichever way you look at it, it was a lousy way to go about it, but that's what jealousy does for you. If I couldn't have you myself *he* certainly wasn't going to! Only even that didn't seem to reach you, so I had to find another way.' His voice roughened again at the memory. 'That was when I knew I couldn't carry it on any further. I had to get out before I got singed too badly. Only it was too late already.'

'It still is.' She pulled away from him and stuck her hands in the pockets of her robe, throat aching. 'You don't love me, Clay. Not the way I see it.'

'Perhaps that's because you're seeing it the way *you'd* have liked it to be. I'm not trying to pretend it's an ideal way to start off, but it's what we make of it from here that counts.' He made a sudden impatient sound in his throat. 'Oh, to hell with talking round it! There's a better way of showing you.'

There was, and it was devastating. When he paused for breath she could only cling to him, face against his chest, heart galloping. She had to believe him now. No man could act that kind of emotion. And he was right —there was no changing what was already past. It had to be accepted and then forgotten. What was important was here and now; loving and being loved. They could build on that.

'Say it, Alex,' he said in her ear. 'I want to hear you say it.'

She laughed, lifting her head to look at him. 'Say what? That I want you? You already know it.'

He shook her, eyes glinting dangerously. 'Say it!'

'All right.' Her voice had a tremulous note. 'I love you, Clay. I love you, I want you and I can't do without you. You're a brute, and I'm sure you're going to be terrible to live with, but I'll have to put up with that.'

He was laughing, gathering her close. 'I'll try to reform.' He smoothed her hair and kissed her temple, found her mouth again and hardened into passion, rousing her to a response which left her shaken and tumultuous. 'I want you now,' he said softly. 'Not tomorrow or next week. Now! Are you going to make me wait till you've got that ring on your finger?'

'Yes, I am.' She tried to make it firm. 'It may be old-fashioned, but that's what I am.'

'Supposing I say no?'

'Then I'd say that any man who can't wait a few weeks can't love very deeply.'

'That's putting me in a cleft stick. Anyway, you can forget about waiting weeks. We're going to tie that knot as soon as we can arrange it. I want everyone on this damned ship to know you're spoken for before some other guy starts getting ideas. You can see Christmas week out, then I'll see your contract is terminated.'

It was a sticky moment; Alex let instinct guide her. '*You'll* terminate it?'

He shrugged lightly. 'It had to come out some time, I suppose. Maybe it will explain things if I tell you my grandfather founded the Connaught Line, using my grandmother's maiden name. We went public years ago, of course, but my father retained enough shares to give him a controlling interest. They came to me when he died.'

'Then why are you doing this job?'

'Because I like it. I'll drop it when we're married and start managing you instead.' He laughed. 'You realise Eva is going to take all the credit for bringing us together?'

'She had a good try.' Alex hesitated before saying it. 'Do you really think she's going to offer me a contract with Bensons?'

'Without a doubt.'

'And you won't mind?'

He shook his head. 'I'm not going to get in the way of your career. I might even take Eva up on an offer she made me to go in with her. She might seem a pretty resilient character, but she's also a lonely one.' He looked at her and his voice softened. 'Happy?'

'More than you could possibly guess.' She drew slightly away from him, wanting him to stay with her but conscious of other immediate claims. 'Clay, you must go and see how June is.'

'She's in good hands, and she has her husband with her.' He pulled her back to him firmly, pushing aside her robe to press his lips to the hollow between her breasts, his hands sliding round her to lift her up and into his arms. Alex felt the desire rising in her, sharp and sweet, undermining resolve until she knew it was either now or never.

'Clay ...' she whispered. 'Please ...'

'I know.' He lifted his head, face rueful. 'I'm not playing fair. And you were right, a little self-denial will do me good. I'd better go while I can still see it that way. Only don't expect too much. I'll almost certainly forget any promises the minute we get together again.' He set her back on her feet but didn't let her go, holding her there lightly in front of him with an expression that almost finished her. 'God,' he said thickly, 'I never imagined feeling this way about any woman. I don't deserve you, but I've got you and I'm going to keep you. Maybe it won't be roses all the way—we're too much alike in temperament for that—but whatever fights we have in the future they can't be any worse than the ones we've already had. And,' with a glint, 'I'll know how to deal with you. Think you're going to be able to take it?'

No, Alex thought, it wasn't going to be an easy path to tread. Clay was going to insist upon being the dominant partner and she wasn't always going to be able to accept it that way. He would be possessive about her, yet probably see no reason why she should be the same way about him. But set against all that would be the knowledge that he loved her—that he'd started to love her even believing what he had believed about her. And providing she had that love she could learn to handle the rest.

'I'll take it,' she said.

Best Seller Romances

Romances you have loved

Mills & Boon Best Seller Romances are the
love stories that have proved particularly
popular with our readers. They really are "back
by popular demand." These are the six titles
to look out for this month.

BOUND FOR MARANDOO
by Kerry Allyne

'I'm looking for a husband who can afford to keep me in a manner
to which I'm *un*accustomed!' Jade had declared jokingly when
asked why she had travelled all the way to the Australian Outback.
Unfortunately Tory McGrath, who was going to be her boss,
heard her words and took them seriously!

REILLY'S WOMAN
by Janet Dailey

Leah's introduction to Reilly Smith hadn't been a very encouraging
one, and he hadn't appeared to her in a very impressive light. All
the same, she found herself wondering just what kind of a man he
was. She was to get her opportunity to find out, when they
crash-landed in the Nevada desert . . .

Mills & Boon

NOT A MARRYING MAN
by Roberta Leigh

How could one like a man who made no secret of the fact that he regarded women as playmates and disliked having them in business? For Sara Vale was very far from being a hardened career woman, much as she loved her job, and she resented Bruno Lyn's attitude. Then her resentment changed to love – but where would that get her? For she was still, in Bruno's eyes, the last woman he would think of in a romantic light . . .

CHARADE IN WINTER
by Anne Mather

Alix had her own reasons for wanting the job at Darkwater Hall, and they weren't calculated to appeal to her employer, Oliver Morgan. So she kept them secret until she arrived in remote Northumberland – only to find that the job she had been hired to do didn't exist, and that Oliver Morgan's disturbing presence could easily upset all her plans.

ACROSS A CROWDED ROOM
by Lilian Peake

Lisette was struggling to keep the family business going against overwhelming odds – but it looked as if soon she was going to have to admit defeat. One man could help her – Rosco Hamden – but his price would be a high one. Could she bring herself to pay it?

CARIBBEAN ENCOUNTER
by Kay Thorpe

Alex's job – three months as resident singer on board a Caribbean cruise liner – sounded glamorous and fun. And so it might have been, had it not been for the undisguised hostility of the dour Cruise Director, Clay Anderson.

the rose of romance